Kill Me, Help Me, Love Me, Save Me.

By Paisley Russell

Prologue

Tears streamed down Samantha's face as she stood at the edge of the pavement watching all of the cars speed by and trying to figure out which would be the best option for her. She knew she needed to pick a fast vehicle that would hopefully cause the most damage and give her an instant and painless death so that she wouldn't end up lying in the middle of the road screaming out in pain whilst she slowly bled out.

When she'd considered the different methods she could use, stepping into traffic had seemed like the most simple idea, but now that she was only seconds away from putting her plan into action, she suddenly felt a lot more intimidated than she'd thought she would.

She didn't want something to go wrong or for her plan to backfire and she be left with permanent brain damage instead of just dying and getting her misery over with. Not only that, but as she'd stood there she'd started to worry about how what she did would affect the driver of whichever car she ended up choosing. Would they get blamed for killing her? Or would the suicide note she'd left in her flat along with any witnesses in the other cars be enough to show that the person wasn't at fault?

Even if they didn't get arrested or anything, she still had to consider how they could be affected psychologically after helping to kill her. Would they be scarred for life? Would they blame *themselves*?

Samantha would never know, but she hated the idea of causing problems that she wouldn't be around to help fix. She'd always heard people talk about how suicide was selfish, and she'd thought that herself until recently, so she didn't want to be remembered for taking the easy way out and leaving a mess behind her for other people to fix.

Suicide had always been something that she didn't understand. She couldn't wrap her head around how a person could get to a point where they thought that all hope was lost and their only option was to end their own life. There was always someone they could talk to, she'd thought. Someone who could help them and give them hope again. How hard could it possibly be to admit that something was wrong and go and talk to a doctor?

It turned out it was a lot harder than she'd first imagined.

The clock struck midday somewhere in the distance and she realised she'd been standing there for over twenty minutes, lost in her troubled thoughts and trying to talk herself out of doing something at the same time as urging herself to do it quickly so that her pain could finally be over and she could be free.

"Come on Samantha," she muttered to herself. "Don't be scared. This is the only way."

Feeling a newfound determination, she brushed the tears off her face and straightened her shoulders, eyeing the road with an intense, watchful gaze as she waited for the right car to appear.

Finally it was there.

A sleek, bulky black car rounded a corner and then drove towards her at about sixty miles per hour. It was a straight stretch of road with no traffic lights to make people slow down.

The perfect place.

As she watched the car getting closer, a sudden sense of peace washed over her and she felt an almost excited tingling in her stomach which told her she was making the right choice.

She closed her eyes for a second and whispered, "Goodbye," before stepping into the road at exactly the right time and bracing herself for the impact she knew was coming.

Chapter One

The noise of the traffic stopped abruptly as Samantha landed with a dull thud on the solid asphalt and sharp sparks of pain started radiating from her skin.

"Oh my god. Oh shit. Are you okay?"

She was aware of footsteps pounding over to where she lay, but was unable to open her eyes or find any words to respond.

"Wake up. Please." A warm hand pressed against her neck to search for a pulse and then she heard the man who'd been talking let out a relieved sigh. "Thank god. You're alive." She listened as he rang for an ambulance and discussed her and her condition with other people that must have crowded around to see what was going on.

"She walked in front of your car. I saw her. She was crying."

"Do you think she did it on purpose?"

"Was she trying to kill herself?"

"Is she going to die?"

The man's voice spoke again. "No. She'll be fine, I think. Luckily I've got good reflexes so I braked as soon as I saw her and didn't end up hitting her that hard."

The crowd started asking more questions but Samantha zoned them out, unable to think about anything except her aching body and the words running through her mind on a continuous loop.

It didn't work.

I'm still here.

Chapter Two

Samantha fell asleep at some point on the drive to the hospital and didn't wake up again until what felt like a significant amount of time later.

There was a nurse fussing with her bedsheets when she finally managed to open her eyelids, and she let out a small moan as she felt a twinge of pain in her side as she was shifted about.

"Oh, sorry," the nurse said with an abnormally wide smile once she saw that Samantha was awake. "Did I hurt you?"

Samantha shook her head and cleared her throat. "Not too much." Her eyes flicked around the room, taking in the stark white walls and beeping machines that had wires leading into her skin. "Are my mum and dad here? Do they know what I did?"

The nurse's expression turned sympathetic. "Yeah, they know. They were here all afternoon but had to go home a little while ago because visiting hours are over."

Samantha sighed, trying to imagine what her parents might have to say to her once she saw them again. She wondered if anyone had been to her flat and found her goodbye note, or if they were all completely clueless about why she'd walked in front of that car.

"What happens now?" she couldn't help but ask, knowing it would never be as easy as her being sent home to potentially try the same thing again in a couple of days.

"A doctor will come and speak to you tomorrow and then decide what to do next," the nurse told her. "But, for now, you should get some more sleep. Your body has been through a massive trauma and sleep will help it to start recovering."

"How bad is it? Is there any permanent damage?"

"No, thank god. You've got a couple of fractures, and a lot of cuts and bruises, but other than that you escaped reasonably well."

"Great."

The nurse didn't respond to Samantha's sarcastic tone and instead just gave her a reassuring smile, told her to press the button beside the bed if her pain medication started to wear off, and then stepped out of the room to let her rest.

"Samantha!"

She almost groaned as she saw her mum and dad burst through the door and rush over to her bed, looking down at her worriedly.

"How are you feeling?"

Samantha winced as her mum, Elizabeth, stroked a hand over a bandage on her forehead. "I'm sore."

"Oh love."

The three of them shared a brief, awkward silence before her dad, Joe, finally addressed the issue at the forefront of everyone's minds.

"Samantha, why did you do this? Why didn't you tell us how you were feeling?"

"I don't know." Her voice sounded small when she spoke; like she was still a little girl getting told off by her parents. "Did you find my note?"

Her mum sighed. "Yeah. We went to your flat to get you some clothes and toiletries for while you're here, and we found it."

It was embarrassing to know that they had read her most intimate thoughts and feelings, and she couldn't help but feel guilty for burdening them with her problems.

"I'm sorry."

"Ssh, love," her mum said. "You don't have to apologise. We're just glad you're still here. We'll make sure you get the help you need."

"Yeah, the doctor said he's going to evaluate you later, and that Wardell guy said he'd like to speak to you as well and see if you'd like his help."

"Wardell?" Samantha frowned, not recognising the name. "Who's Wardell?"

"The guy who hit you," her dad explained. "In some ways, it was actually quite lucky that you decided to walk in front of a therapist's car. He works at a private clinic near here and he's offered to give you discounted sessions, as long as you're comfortable with that. It would mean you wouldn't have to join a six month waiting list. You could start getting help straight away."

"Oh. So, did he give you his number or something?" She remembered the concerned sounding man at her side whilst she was lying on the road waiting for the ambulance, and wondered how uncomfortable it would be to have to meet him again and actually see his face.

"Yeah. He was at the hospital yesterday when we arrived and he gave us his card and told us to call once you were ready. Isn't that kind?"

"Yeah, I suppose."

It still didn't mean that she wanted to tell him all her private thoughts, and she definitely didn't like the idea of paying for the privilege to do so.

Deciding to worry about it later, Samantha tried to change the subject. "Did you tell my work what happened?"

Her mum gave her a sad smile. "Yeah, we had to. They said to pass on their best wishes and to keep them updated and let them know when you think you'll be back."

Samantha wanted to roll her eyes at the predictable, uncaring response from her employers. She was surprised they hadn't asked if she could at least work from home for the time being or told her to send proof that she was really in hospital and had really tried to kill herself.

A knock on the door interrupted them and they turned to see the nurse from the previous day pop her head into the room. "Hi guys. The doctor is here to speak to Samantha. Are you okay giving them some privacy?"

"We'll see you later," her dad said as he and her mum followed the nurse out to the waiting room.

The door barely shut for a second before it swung back open and a stern looking, grey haired woman entered.

"Hello Samantha, I'm Doctor Walls," she said in an emotionless tone; taking a seat beside the bed and pulling a notebook and pen from her handbag. "So, tell me how you're feeling."

Chapter Three

Doctor Walls left the room over an hour later, after Samantha had sufficiently made a fool out of herself by crying her eyes out and revealing the details of her muddled mind.

The headteacher-like woman hadn't commented on any of the things that Samantha had told her. Instead, she'd only nodded her head or scribbled something down in her book before asking another probing question.

Samantha could hear the doctor's low murmur just outside her door, discussing her with her parents and no doubt filling them in on whatever diagnosis she had made after their talk.

She knew she was correct when she saw the false looking smiles on her mum and dad's faces as they walked back into the room.

"Hey, how did it go?" her mum asked.

Samantha shrugged, not wanting to give too much away. "Fine."

"Do you feel any better after talking to someone about everything?"

"Not really."

Her dad sighed heavily and exchanged a meaningful look with her mum, as if they both thought that she was being purposely awkward. "Why not?"

"I don't know. I just didn't feel comfortable around her."

"But she said you opened up a lot?"

"Yeah, I did. But then her reactions to everything I said made me feel stupid." She struggled to explain exactly what she meant without making it look like she was refusing help. "I don't think I need a therapist anyway," she said decisively. "Doctor Walls said she was going to prescribe me some tablets. Surely they'll be enough to help me?"

Her mum and dad didn't look convinced but they thankfully didn't get a chance to try and change her mind because the nurse came in again to tell them that visiting hours were over and they would have to go home.

"We'll see you tomorrow love." Her mum placed a kiss on her forehead. "Call me if you want to talk about anything in the meantime."

Samantha was given her first tablet to take the next morning.

"We won't give you a full prescription just yet," the nurse said as she handed her a plastic cup of water. "The doctor said she's not sure if she can trust you with more than one at a time."

She tried to make it sound like a joke, but Samantha wasn't amused. It was embarrassing to know that people thought she was so unstable; even though she'd really given them no reason to think differently after she'd chosen to walk in front of a car.

"You might feel a bit sick at first, but just drink lots of water and it should pass once your system absorbs the tablet."

"Okay." Samantha shuddered as the little white pill slid down her throat, leaving a strange taste on her tongue which she quickly tried to wash away by taking a big gulp of her water. Once it was done, she turned back to her nurse. "Do you know when I'll be getting discharged?"

"It should hopefully be tomorrow, I think. You're healing well so far, and there's not much more we can do for you here. *Physically* I mean."

"Right."

She was relieved to hear that she would get to go home soon. Although there were many times when she hated being alone in her flat with no company except her whirring thoughts, it was still a better option than the clinical surroundings she'd had for the last couple of days, and the feeling that she was being constantly watched, as if she was going to jump straight from one suicide attempt to another.

The truth was that she wasn't even considering trying to harm herself again any time soon because she'd begun to wonder if the reason she hadn't died might be because she wasn't *supposed* to.

Maybe the universe was telling her to keep powering on.

Maybe there could be a different ending to her story.

Chapter Four

"Wardell's here to talk to you," Samantha's dad announced unexpectedly the next day.

"What?" She felt herself pale as a nervous feeling started in her stomach. "Why? I didn't say I wanted to speak to him."

"Yes, I know. But we thought it was worth a try because you said you didn't like the doctor yesterday, so we hoped he might be better. Plus, he wanted to see you. He was worried about you, so we thought it would be nice if the both of you could meet properly. He did save your life, after all."

"But-" How could she explain that the idea of meeting the man who'd knocked her over was humiliating? Thinking quickly, she came up with another argument. "You said he works at a private clinic. I wouldn't be able to afford the sessions with him."

Her dad waved his hand dismissively. "Don't worry about that. Me and your mum will pay."

Clearly seeing the indecision still on Samantha's face, her mum added, "Come on. What's the harm in just meeting him for a few minutes? He seems like a nice guy. I reckon he'd be easy for you to talk to. But if you don't like him, then you don't have to have any more sessions."

Samantha considered her options but couldn't think of a way to change her mum and dad's minds.

"Fine," she sighed. "I'll meet him."

She braced herself as she heard footsteps approaching her room a short while later, once her parents had left to go and get some food from the hospital cafe.

When Wardell strolled through the door and came to a stop at the foot of her bed, Samantha's mouth dropped open at his unexpected attractiveness.

He was younger than she'd thought he would be. Up until then, she had imagined a man in his sixties, but instead he seemed to only be in his late thirties at the most; something which she only guessed because of the small lines around his eyes and the few grey hairs in amongst the brown. His body, however, looked like it could belong to someone ten years younger. He clearly looked after himself, and she couldn't help but feel embarrassed about having someone who was potentially ten years older than her be so much fitter than she was.

Wardell's eyes lit up as he smiled at her, and she could immediately understand why her parents had kept saying he seemed nice. There was something about the way he stared at her and his body language which just made him seem friendly and open; like someone who was willing to hear all of your problems.

She wondered if he had always been that way, or if he had transformed over the years because of his job as a therapist.

"Hi Samantha," he said in a voice that already sounded soothing. "It's good to see you again."

She automatically screwed up her face at the reminder of their first meeting. "Well, my eyes were closed last time so I didn't actually see you."

He let out a small chuckle. "So how are you feeling?"

It was probably the hundredth time somebody had asked her that question since she'd first been admitted to the hospital, and she was getting tired of always giving the same blunt answer.

"I'm fine."

"Good." He moved a few steps forward and gestured to the chair beside her bed. "Do you mind if I sit down for a bit?"

"No, it's okay."

"Thanks." He took a seat. "So, did your mum and dad tell you why I'm here?"

"Kind of." She was aware she was behaving like a child instead of the twenty seven year old woman she really was, but her awkwardness was making her unable to say more than just a few words at a time.

"I've been thinking about you a lot since the other day. I've had a lot of patients who've tried to commit suicide, but I've never actually witnessed anyone doing it. And I've never been the person who almost killed them before."

Samantha felt her cheeks heat, and she avoided his eyes as she replied. "Sorry about that. You don't have to feel guilty or anything. It wasn't your fault."

"I know." He sighed. "But I still feel like it's my responsibility to try and help you now. I know this might sound stupid, but I feel like there was a reason why you just so happened to choose *my* car to walk in front of. Surely it can't just be a coincidence that I happen to be a therapist who specialises in anxiety and OCD which, from what your parents told me, is exactly what you're struggling with."

Samantha had to admit that there was some sense to his words. It *was* strange that she had chosen his car out of the dozens of ones that had driven past her that day.

"Would you like me to help you?" Wardell asked when she didn't respond straight away. "I've already discussed everything with your mum and dad, but I think it would be best if we have two sessions a week to start with, on a Monday and a Friday. The first appointment would just be a sort of initial consultation where I get a bit of background from you about what exactly you're struggling with and when it all started. We can go at your pace, so you wouldn't have to talk about anything too personal unless you were fully comfortable doing so. And, of course, if for some reason you thought the sessions weren't working, or you wanted to go and see someone else, you could stop at any time. So what do you think?"

Samantha finally allowed herself to meet his gaze again, seeing the sincerity there which immediately made her shoulders relax. The intense way he was watching her spoke of confidence and a calming nature, and she had the sudden thought that if anyone was capable of fixing her, it would be him.

"Alright," she said quietly, still sounding reluctant. "I'll give it a go."

"Great!" Wardell smiled widely, showing off a dimple in his left cheek, and making her chest flutter in a way she knew was probably not appropriate. "This is the start of a new chapter for you Samantha. I promise."

Chapter Five

Samantha was finally allowed to go home the next afternoon.

Her mum and dad gave her a lift back to her flat but once they were parked outside, she told them she wanted to be alone for a while.

"Are you sure?" her mum asked, looking concerned. "I was thinking we could come in to watch a film and then maybe order a takeaway later."

Samantha pulled a face. "No offence, but do you mind if we do that tomorrow or something? I just want to have a shower and chill out for a bit."

They both still seemed unsure about the idea and exchanged a worried look, making Samantha sigh as she realised what they must have been thinking.

"I'm not going to do anything, don't worry. I'll call you later if you want, to let you know that I'm okay."

That seemed to reassure them slightly and so they waved her off before getting back in their car and driving away once they saw she'd got inside safely.

As she entered her flat and looked around at the familiar space, Samantha remembered the moment she'd last stood in that same spot, gazing wistfully at all of her belongings before she left for what she'd thought would be the final time.

Walking into her bedroom, she saw that her note was no longer on the bed and made a mental note to ask her parents if they had thrown it away or kept it for themselves.

Personally, she didn't ever want to see it again.

She spent the next few hours under a blanket on her couch, watching rubbish TV and doing her best to distract herself so that the intrusive thoughts that had been itching at the corners of her mind didn't have a chance to crowd in.

However, once she was in bed that night and trying to fall asleep, there was nothing left to occupy her brain and so the questions soon started.

Did I lock the door?

Did I leave the oven on?

Did I leave the heater on and could it now be setting fire to the flat?

It was a never ending loop.

Samantha fought against the urges to check for as long as possible, but eventually she knew that the doubts weren't going to go away and so she climbed out of bed and allowed herself just one check.

Everything was locked and switched off.

She curled back under her duvet and shut her eyes, but a couple of minutes later the questions started again.

Did I accidentally unlock the door and turn everything on when I was trying to check them?

Have I made everything worse by trying to reassure myself?

"Just one more time," she muttered to herself before climbing back out of bed.

She must have been up and down more than a dozen times over the next couple of hours, attempting to settle her mind with one last check, but ultimately finding something else to worry about instead.

When she finally fell into a restless sleep, there were tears running down her cheeks.

The tablets aren't working, a voice said at the back of her brain. *The thoughts are still here. I'm never going to get better.*

Chapter Six

By Monday, Samantha was almost excited about going to her first therapy session with Wardell. Not because he would be nice to look at, but because she'd had a tough few days and was desperate to try anything that might help to fix her before she ended up doing something stupid again.

"Do you want me to come in and sit in the waiting room?" her mum asked as she pulled the car to a stop outside the fancy looking office building.

"No, it's okay," Samantha told her. "Just go for a coffee or something and I'll ring you when I get out."

Turning away from the car, she walked through the sliding glass door and up to the front desk which had an overly cheerful receptionist sitting behind it; someone who was probably supposed to be reassuring for the patients that came in the building, but who was only intimidating Samantha at that moment in time.

"Good morning, do you have an appointment?"

"Err yeah. With…Wardell." She realised that she only knew his first name, and hoped there wasn't another Doctor Wardell in the building. "My name's Samantha, if that helps."

The receptionist scanned her eyes across her computer screen and then nodded to herself as she found the appropriate appointment. "Okay, no problem. So just go through that door and up the stairs and take a seat in the waiting room. I'll let Doctor Briggs know you're here."

"Thanks."

As she made her way to the first floor, Samantha was glad that she'd decided to dress up for the appointment by putting on one of her smart black work dresses and a low pair of heels. Although she knew Wardell was already aware of her problems, she'd wanted to look well put together on the outside so that it made her feel internally stronger.

Taking a seat in a comfortable black armchair, she pulled a book out of her handbag, expecting to have a long wait until she got called in like she usually did when she went to see any kind of doctor. Instead, however, she jumped in surprise when a door to her right suddenly opened and Wardell appeared with a warm, welcoming smile on his face. "Samantha. Hi. Good to see you."

"Oh. Hi," she stuttered, still in shock that he was there for her so soon, when she hadn't even had a chance to relax yet.

She hesitantly walked into his treatment room, hearing him close the thick wooden door behind them as she eyed his large desk and the luxurious couch positioned in front of it.

"Take a seat," he said. "Would you like a drink?"

"Erm." She suddenly realised how dry her mouth was and doubted she would be able to talk much if she didn't wet it in some way. "Can I have a glass of water?"

"Of course." There was silence between them both for a moment whilst he poured some drinks, and then he sat down in his desk chair and stared at her in the intense way she remembered from their first meeting.

"So, first things first, I've got a couple of questionnaires I'd like you to complete." He slid some sheets of paper across his desk and held out a pen for her. "Make sure you answer everything honestly. Don't be embarrassed, okay?"

Samantha nodded and took the pen with a trembling hand.

She was aware of Wardell watching her as she answered each question, but didn't let it distract her or stop her from telling the truth about how often the things listed affected her.

"Here you go," she said less than ten minutes later, handing everything back to him.

He ran his gaze across the papers, raising his eyebrows slightly every now and again, but thankfully making no comment.

"Okay." He quickly typed something into his laptop and then met her eyes once more. "So when did all this start?"

"Alright. I think we're done for today. I know we didn't really go into too much, but like I told you at the hospital, this was just a sort of evaluation. I just wanted a bit of background to everything so I can make a proper treatment plan for you. We'll start properly on Friday."

Samantha smiled awkwardly, feeling uncomfortable about everything she had revealed over the last hour even though it hadn't been much in the grand scheme of things.

She'd been glad to find that she didn't cry again when telling him the details of her anxiety, and she wondered if it was because she was getting used to speaking about it or just because Wardell was so much easier to talk to than Doctor Walls had been.

"I'll walk you out," he said with a smile, gesturing for her to go first. "How are you finding your tablets, by the way? Have you experienced any sickness?"

"I felt sick for the first two days, but it seems to have gone now. I don't think they're working though."

Wardell made a sympathetic face. "Unfortunately, they won't work this soon. It usually takes four to six weeks for them to start having an effect."

"Great," she muttered sarcastically.

"In the meantime, if you ever have any low moments, or you find yourself stuck in a cycle that you can't break and you feel like you need to talk to someone, here." He held out one of his business cards. "You can call me any time."

"Really?"

He smiled his perfect smile. "Of course. I'm here to help."

"Okay. Cool." She fiddled with the strap of her handbag nervously. "Well, I'll see you on Friday then."

Wardell nodded. "See you on Friday. And good luck with your first day back at work tomorrow."

The reminder made her stomach hurt.

Chapter Seven

Samantha thought she might actually throw up as she got the lift up to her company's office the next day.

She hadn't liked her job for the whole three years she'd worked there, but she was too shy and scared of the unknown so had never bothered to look for something else to do.

She'd purposely arrived half an hour early so that she wouldn't have the embarrassment of walking past everyone else's desks and would instead hopefully blend into the background with people perhaps not even realising she was there.

And, of course, there was always the chance that they hadn't noticed she'd been gone in the first place. After all, her colleagues barely spoke to her except for when they needed something doing, and she rarely spoke in general so she wasn't exactly a big presence there.

Loading up her laptop, she busied herself with catching up on emails and then trying to find the missing items from her desk which people had clearly 'borrowed' and then not put back.

When people started to filter in, she sat back down again and kept her gaze locked on her screen, but quickly became aware of eyes on her and knew that her boss must have told everyone about what she'd done.

So much for confidentiality, she thought.

Of course nobody cared enough to actually ask how she was or say some kind of fake 'glad to have you back'. Instead, they only stared at her warily, as if she was some kind of freak who they expected to stand up and start slashing at her wrists at any given moment.

Doing her best to ignore everyone, Samantha put her earphones in, turned her music on as loud as she could bear, and buried herself in her work.

"How's work been?" Wardell asked her at their appointment on Friday afternoon. She'd had to rush there straight from the office so was still red faced and sweaty by the time she sank onto his couch and he clicked on his pen.

"Awful," she said automatically, scrunching her face up at just the thought of how boring and tense the last four days had been.

"Why's that?"

"I hate the job. I hate the place. I hate the people."

"Why don't you find a new job then?"

"Because I have no idea what I'd want to do, and I hate filling out applications and going for interviews, and chances are the next place would be just as bad. All my other jobs have been."

He raised his eyebrows as if he didn't believe her. "They've *all* been bad?"

"Yeah."

"Why?"

"Because people never like me."

Again, he looked doubtful. "No one has ever liked you?"

"Nope. Not even in school."

He typed something into his laptop and then folded his arms on his desk, giving her his full attention. "Surely you've got some friends?"

"No. None."

"Why do you think that is?"

"Mostly because people think I'm boring. But also because I'm a bit of a loner." She found it a lot easier to be open with him when the topic didn't involve her mental health. Not directly, anyway.

Wardell smiled slightly. "If it makes you feel better, I'm a bit of a loner as well. And just because you might be different compared to the other people you've come across in life, it doesn't mean you're boring."

"Thanks. Can you come to my work and tell my colleagues that?"

"If you want me to." He gave her a teasing look, but then his expression suddenly turned serious again, as if he'd told himself that he shouldn't joke around with her. "Er, anyway, what about your relationship with your family? Do you get on well with your mum and dad?"

Samantha shrugged. "Yeah. Most of the time."

"Do you have any siblings?"

"No. I'm an only child."

He nodded consideringly. "Okay, and what about romantic relationships? Have you had many of them?"

The question made her shift in her seat as she quickly became uncomfortable again. "Um, not really. Just a couple."

"And how long did they last?"

She shrugged, hating having to admit just how inexperienced she was, especially when she was talking to a good looking guy who probably got loads of attention. "I think the longest was about seven weeks."

He looked surprised, but did his best to hide it. "Only seven weeks? Why's that?"

"I don't know." She let out an awkward laugh. "I think guys tend to get bored of me once they've got what they wanted."

"You mean sex?" he asked bluntly.

"Yeah." Samantha cleared her throat. "Um, not to be rude, but why do we have to talk about this?"

"Sorry. I'm just trying to find out more about you. A lot of the time our past relationships can affect our lives long after the actual break ups."

"Awesome," she muttered. "But, no offence, I've already figured out that my lack of friends, lack of boyfriends and stuff like being bullied in school has caused my mental health problems. I didn't exactly need a therapist to tell me that."

Wardell eyed her thoughtfully. "You were bullied in school as well?"

"Oh god." She let out a groan, wishing she'd never said anything. "Yes, I was. And yes, it's affected me throughout my life. Do I really need to tell you any more than that? It's a bit embarrassing."

"Sorry," he said again, giving her a sympathetic smile that she knew must be used on all his patients. "How about this? I'll tell you a bit about my personal life, if you want? Will that make you feel more comfortable?"

Samantha wasn't sure that it would, but she couldn't help but be intrigued by his offer and so agreed to go along with it. "Okay then. Tell me about your relationships. Are you married? Do you have kids?"

He chuckled. "No. I'm single and childless. I *was* engaged about ten years ago though."

She raised her eyebrows. "How old are you?"

"I'm thirty eight."

That made him eleven years older than her. "What went wrong?"

"I found out she'd been cheating on me since before I even proposed."

"Wow." She struggled to think of an appropriate response to what he'd just revealed. "So, have you not met anyone since then that you wanted to marry?"

"Unfortunately, no. I've dated a few women, but it's never turned into anything serious."

Samantha tried to recreate one of the concerned looks he always gave her. "Have you psychoanalysed yourself for why that might be? Do you not trust women anymore?"

Wardell laughed loudly and an unfamiliar look appeared in his eyes. "No, I've not got any problems trusting women. I've just not met the right person yet." Samantha's face grew warm as he watched her intently. "Thanks for caring so much though," he added in a sarcastic tone. "Can we go back to talking about you now?"

Wardell walked her out again at the end of her session. The receptionist had already gone home so her desk was empty, and Samantha wondered if they were the last two people in the building all together.

The thought made her nervous for some reason.

"What are you doing tonight then?" Wardell asked conversationally. "Any plans?"

"Nope. Just staying in and reading probably. What about you?"

"I'm going out for a drink with a couple of my mates."

Samantha frowned. "I thought you said you were a loner?"

"I said I'm a bit of a loner," he clarified. "But I still have a handful of friends."

"Fair enough."

They stopped at the door and turned to face each other.

"Well, thanks then," Samantha said as she absentmindedly began to scratch at one of the scabbed over cuts that were still on her arm. "I'll see you on Monday."

"Yeah. Have a good weekend." Wardell suddenly reached out and placed his hand over hers. "Stop picking that. It'll scar."

She was so distracted by the sensation of their skin touching that it took her a couple of seconds to answer.

"Sorry, she said stupidly, ducking her head down to avoid his gaze. "Bye then."

She hurried out of the door and didn't allow herself to turn around and take one last look at the man who had just caused such an unexpected reaction in her.

Chapter Eight

"Is it true you tried to kill yourself?"

Samantha paused in pouring herself a glass of water from the machine in the office kitchen, and turned to find her colleague watching her with a sort of fascinated expression on his face.

She'd known the question would be asked eventually because people were naturally nosey, but she hadn't expected to be suddenly ambushed in the kitchen first thing on a Monday morning when she was only trying to get herself a drink.

"Err, yeah," she said quietly to the guy whose name she didn't even know. "But I don't really want to talk about it."

Ignoring her request, he began to ask her how she was feeling and what getting hit by a car had been like, but she ignored him and left the room. As she walked away, she almost smiled as she heard him call her a 'rude bitch' but she felt as though she didn't even have the energy to lift her lips.

She'd had a difficult weekend.

Friday night had been manageable because she'd been so distracted with memories of her appointment with Wardell and then had decided to have an early night; but when she woke up on Saturday, she knew immediately that it was going to be a struggle.

First of all, it had taken her over half an hour to just get out of bed. She'd woken with what was becoming a common thought in her mind: that there was something from the night before that she needed to remember, but had forgotten it whilst she'd been asleep.

After going through a variety of options for things that the 'forgotten memory' could relate to, she'd finally felt comfortable with accepting that there was nothing to remember; or that, even if there was, it obviously wasn't important.

The rest of her weekend had gotten even worse from there. It had been one constant stream of thoughts or worries that she couldn't get out of her mind unless she talked herself through each one for sometimes up to an hour.

She hated her life being like that, and was getting frustrated that her tablets still didn't seem to have started working, but she had finally accepted having another couple of wasted days which would hopefully be over soon, and persevered through the rest of her Sunday before going to bed at only seven o' clock.

All in all, Samantha wouldn't call it a success, and that was why she was in no mood to entertain the horrible idiots that she worked with by giving them more ammunition to make fun of her about.

The day passed reasonably quickly and she found herself actually relieved to be on the bus and heading towards her therapy appointment instead of stuck at her desk doing tasks she really didn't care about.

As she walked up to the now familiar building, she felt her heartbeat growing faster, but surprisingly not because of fear.

The truth was that she was *excited* about seeing Wardell again. Although nothing had actually happened on Friday night, and he'd simply just been stopping her from picking her scabs, she couldn't deny that his touch had affected her in some way, and she now felt herself developing a crush on her therapist.

That's probably not healthy, she admitted to herself. *But it's not like I'm going to ask him out or try to kiss him or anything.*

And anyway, if fancying Wardell made her want to actually go to her therapy sessions, was it really a problem?

She thought not.

Chapter Nine

There was somebody in the waiting room when she arrived.

For her past two sessions, she had sat there alone and Wardell had come out to fetch her within a couple of minutes; but of course the one time there was a random man in there eyeing her curiously as he clearly wondered what her problems were, Wardell took almost ten minutes to appear.

"Samantha, come in," Wardell said with a smile once his door finally opened.

She rushed in immediately, feeling oddly relieved once she was hidden away from the other human being who now knew she was seeing a therapist.

"How was your weekend?" Wardell asked her as he poured her usual glass of water and took a seat behind his desk.

Samantha considered whether to lie or not, but then decided it was probably best to tell the truth to the man who was trying to fix her brain.

"It was awful," she admitted. "I spent the whole time worrying about stupid stuff."

"What kind of stuff?"

"Everything." She let out a heavy sigh, feeling overwhelmed at just the memory of it all. "I convinced myself that I might have unlocked my front door without realising so had to keep checking it, I worried I might have left an appliance on, I worried I could have accidentally transferred all of my money out of my account, I worried I might have accidentally text my boss to tell him that I hate him or that I quit." She ran her hands through her hair, pulling anxiously at the roots. "It all sounds so stupid now, but at the time I couldn't concentrate on anything else but those thoughts in my mind, and then I'd try to be strong and not left myself check, but that just made me get more wound up so eventually I gave in and checked, but then I convinced myself I'd checked wrong so then I had to do it over and over again. It was like one endless cycle."

When Samantha finally had to stop talking to take a breath, her cheeks immediately blushed as she realised just how much of her crazy mind she had revealed without meaning to.

She met Wardell's eyes nervously but found him typing into his laptop again, glancing over at her every now and then to give her what was probably supposed to be a reassuring smile.

"Okay. That's good," he said at last, closing the lid of his computer.

"Good?"

The look she gave him made him smile. "No, obviously it's bad that you've been through that, and I'm sorry the weekend was so difficult for you, but it's good that you've told me more about what you're dealing with."

"Do you think I'm a freak?"

He shook his head sternly. "No. Of course not. You're not a freak. There's a lot of people who have similar problems, but they manifest in different ways."

"Really?"

"Yeah. It's common for people to worry that they've somehow missed chunks of time, and that they might have done something and forgotten about it."

"Oh. Okay. Good to know." Just hearing him say that had already made her feel slightly better.

"Have you noticed your tablets working at all yet?"

Samantha scoffed. "No. Not at all."

"Okay, well if you've still not noticed even a slight difference this time next week, I think I'll tell your GP to up your prescription." He wrote a note for himself in the diary on his desk before turning his focus to her again. "So, you had a bad weekend, but how are you feeling today?"

"A bit better, I suppose. Work was a distraction. Even though I hate it, I still like the routine and it keeps my mind busy so..."

Wardell nodded in understanding. "That's good to hear." He cleared his throat and eyed her warily as he asked his next question. "Have you had any more thoughts about...hurting yourself?"

The words made Samantha stiffen. They hadn't really broached the topic of whether she was still suicidal before.

"No, I haven't," she told him honestly. "Even when I was in a real mess this weekend, the idea still didn't come into my mind. I just told myself that the tablets should start working soon so to just wait it out."

"Good." Wardell smiled softly at her. "That's progress."

Chapter Ten

"How was your therapy session?" her mum asked Samantha that night when she went round to her parent's house for dinner.

"It was alright."

"So you think it's helping?"

"Yeah, I think so"

"And you're getting on well with Wardell?"

Samantha nodded. "Yeah. He's a nice guy." She didn't tell them just how *much* she was starting to like him.

"Good." Her mum smiled brightly. "And how's work?"

The questioning went on for the entire time the three of them were eating, and Samantha got to the point where she couldn't wait to leave so that she wouldn't have to talk to anyone about how she was feeling anymore.

"Have you thought about joining some kind of group?" her dad asked as they washed up together after the meal.

Samantha frowned. "What kind of group?"

"A group with other people who struggle with anxiety and depression. We've been looking online and we think it could really help you. You can either go to meetings in person, or just talk online, but basically you just share your problems with people who can relate and maybe make you feel better about things. That way you might not feel so alone."

Samantha hated the idea, and honestly couldn't think of anything worse, but she didn't know how to tell her parents that when they seemed so pleased with themselves for finding a potential solution.

"Um, I'll look into it," she said, hoping that would satisfy them for a while until they finally forgot the idea.

"Why don't you ask Wardell about it on Friday?" her mum suggested. "See what he thinks?"

"Yeah. I will."

Thankfully, Wardell didn't think joining a group was necessary. "I think just these sessions are enough for now," he said. "Eventually, we'll probably go down to just one appointment a week and then maybe you could do something like that, but for now I don't think you'd be very open to talking to a bunch of strangers about what's going on in your head. Am I wrong?"

"No!" Samantha gave him an appreciative smile. "I already thought all of that, but I just wanted to be able to tell mum and dad that even my *therapist* has said I'm not ready to do it."

Wardell laughed. "Well, tell them that it could actually set your recovery back. Having to hear about other people's issues would just make you compare yourself to them, and if they weren't having as hard a time as you then it might make your mood even lower."

"Oh great," Samantha said sarcastically. "That's all I need!" She let out a heavy sigh. "I know they're just trying to help, but they're kind of annoying me with how much they keep fussing. I know it probably sounds really ungrateful, but I just keep thinking that if they cared so much they should have tried to help me years ago."

Wardell cocked his head. "What do you mean?"

"Nothing." She shook her head, wishing she'd never said the words, but unfortunately he didn't let it drop.

"No, that wasn't nothing. What did you mean?"

"Just..." She brushed her hair back behind her ears repetitively. "When I was in school and I was getting bullied, I told them about it but they said that loads of kids have to deal with that kind of stuff so I just had to put up with it. And then when my OCD first started when I was about sixteen, I told my mum about it but she said I was being over dramatic and that liking things to be a certain way didn't mean I had OCD so I needed to just put it to the back of my mind and eventually it would go away. They've known for years how much I struggle with things, and about how lonely I am, but then when I was in the hospital they were acting as if me trying to kill myself came out of nowhere. As if they'd known nothing about it."

Wardell eyed her silently, considering everything she'd just said. "So, do you blame them? Do you think that maybe things wouldn't have gotten so bad if they'd helped you sooner?"

Samantha sighed. "Yeah, maybe. I know that's not fair and that I can't say it's their fault, but they've left me to deal with everything on my own in the past, so it's annoying the hell out of me that they suddenly want to be super parents."

"Maybe they feel guilty?"

"Yeah, I think they do. But they need to realise that trying to force me into making new friends isn't going to solve anything." She put her head in her hands and groaned. "Oh god. I sound horrible. I don't even know what I'm talking about. I'm not even annoyed with them usually." She sat up straight in her chair again. "Ignore me. I'm being irrational."

"Why do you think you're being irrational?"

"Well, don't *you* think I am?"

Wardell shook his head. "It's not for me to say what I think is rational or not. All that matters is that, for you, your parents lack of support in the past has obviously been an issue."

Samantha tried her best to read his expression, wanting to figure out what his true opinion was, but unfortunately he seemed to be an expert at putting on a neutral facade.

"Can we talk about something else?"

"Yeah, if that's what you want."

He suddenly sounded like more of a therapist than usual and she felt herself getting riled up again. "Actually can we just end the session now?"

Wardell's brow furrowed. "What's wrong?"

"Nothing. I just want to go home. I've had a long week."

"Samantha..." He glanced at the clock. "We've still got forty minutes left."

"So I can't leave then? I'm trapped here until you say I can go?" She wasn't sure where her attitude was coming from, but she couldn't stop it.

"No, you're not trapped here. If you really want to leave, you can."

"Awesome." She stood up and began to make her way towards the door, but he spoke again before she could even twist the handle.

"Samantha?"

"What?"

"If you need help this weekend, remember you can always ring me. Okay?"

"Okay."

She pulled open the door and began to march down the stairs, hearing him call out behind her.

"See you on Monday!"

Chapter Eleven

Samantha couldn't shake her strange mood for the rest of that night, but by Saturday afternoon she was feeling like an idiot and regretted everything she'd said to Wardell.

She hated that she could have caused some kind of rift between them which would make future appointments awkward, so in the end decided to give him a call to sort things out and stop it from playing on her mind.

As she held the phone to her ear she began to worry that he might not even answer. Maybe he'd had enough of her and all of her drama and was going to give up on her?

Thankfully, the call connected after only a couple of rings and his deep voice came down the line. "Samantha?"

She couldn't help but notice how wary he sounded and purposely spoke in her most cheerful tone. "Hey! Sorry, are you busy?"

"Err, no. I'm just at home. Is everything okay?"

"Yeah." She let out a long breath. "I was just calling to apologise for how I acted yesterday. I don't know what was wrong with me."

"That's alright. You don't need to apologise. Believe me, I've had worse from patients."

Hearing him refer to her as just a patient stung for some reason, but she ignored the tightness in her chest and continued with her apology. "Well, I couldn't relax because it was bothering me so much. I just wanted to check that you didn't hate me after how rude I was."

Wardell let out a breathy chuckle. "I don't hate you, Samantha. Don't worry. Everyone has bad days sometimes, and with everything else you've got going on in your life at the moment, and with everything you're dealing with in your mind, it's quite normal for you to have the odd outburst."

"Oh. Okay."

She felt better for having spoken to him but now didn't know whether to end the conversation or to continue talking, so she left them in an uncomfortable silence until finally Wardell spoke again.

"What are you up to this weekend? I never got a chance to ask you yesterday."

"Um, nothing. As usual. I might read a bit later."

"And how's your anxiety? Is it bad like last weekend?"

"Er, well, yeah. But that might just be because I was worrying about everything with you. It might get better now I've apologised."

"Do you want to talk about it anyway?"

"Not really."

"Okay."

Samantha worried that he was growing exasperated with her so quickly tried to make things better by changing the subject. "What are *you* doing this weekend? Any dates?"

She wasn't sure why she had asked such a stupid question and immediately wished she could take the words back.

Wardell was obviously surprised by it as well because there was a significant pause before he answered. "No. I've not got a date."

"Oh. Cool." She slapped her palm against her forehead. "Well, I'm gonna go."

"Alright. Try and enjoy the rest of your weekend. And call me if you need anything else."

"Thanks."

She quickly hung up.

Less than twelve hours later, Samantha dialled Wardell's number again.

It was almost two in the morning and she'd been lying awake in bed for hours, struggling to switch her thoughts off enough to fall asleep.

She'd lost count of the amount of times she'd been up and down to check everything in her flat or on her phone, and the longer it had gone on and the more she'd let the intrusive thoughts in, the more wound up she'd got until finally she was in floods of tears.

Although she knew Wardell probably hadn't meant the early hours of the morning when he'd told her to ring at any time, she was so desperate by that point that she didn't stop to think about anything else other than how much she needed his help.

Surprisingly, it didn't take him long to answer, but when he did he sounded extremely groggy. "Hello?"

Samantha tried to hold back a sob. "Wardell?"

He must have heard the tears in her voice because when he spoke again, it was with a sort of urgency. "What's wrong? Are you okay?"

"No. Not really." She let out a choked breath. "I can't sleep. My brain won't shut up."

She heard a rustling through the phone and guessed that Wardell had sat up in bed. "Samantha, have you tried to hurt yourself?"

"No." She wiped her nose on the back of her hand. "But I can't stop checking everything, and I can't relax, and each time I go over stuff it just makes me feel worse instead of helping and I don't know what to do."

Wardell was quiet for a moment, as if thinking about his next words, and when he asked his next question, it was the last thing she had expected him to ever say.

"What's your address?"

Chapter Twelve

It only took Wardell about fifteen minutes to get to her flat. Samantha had done her best to try and calm herself down whilst she waited because she didn't want him to see her tear stained cheeks, red nose, or puffy eyes; but as she took one final look in the mirror after buzzing him into the building, she saw that her efforts hadn't been very successful.

She looked terrible.

Nothing you can do about it now, she thought as she heard light knocking on her front door and rushed to go and answer it before the noise could wake up any of her neighbours.

Wardell's face fell as soon as he saw the state she was in, and he quickly stepped inside and closed the door quietly behind him.

"Are you okay?"

Samantha started to nod her head, but the question made tears start pouring from her eyes once more so in the end it turned into a sort of shake. "No."

He unexpectedly wrapped his arms around her and pulled her close, resting his chin on the top of her head as his hand stroked up and down her back in a comforting rhythm.

It was only then that she remembered she was still in her skimpy pyjama shorts and a vest. She'd been so busy worrying about covering up her crying face that she'd not even thought to change her outfit to something a bit more appropriate.

"Ssh, try and calm down," Wardell said in a soothing tone. "You've got yourself into a right state.

"I know." She was struggling to catch her breath due to how much she was sobbing. "I can barely even remember what started it anymore."

"Let's sit down," Wardell suggested, leading her over to her couch but still keeping an arm around her shoulders and staying close to her side once they were there.

"I'm sorry. For waking you up. This is so embarrassing."

"It's okay. Don't worry about it. I told you to call me whenever you need me."

"I bet your other patients don't do this."

He didn't answer, but she saw a strange, pensive expression on his face for a few moments before he quickly shook it away and got back to business. "That doesn't matter.

I'm going to speak to your GP on Monday, alright? I'm going to get him to give you a higher dose of the tablets. Then they should hopefully start working."

"What if they don't?"

He shrugged. "Then we'll try something else. But I'm not giving up on you. I promise."

After almost another ten minutes, Samantha finally started to quieten down and her tears dried up.

"Feeling better?" Wardell asked, giving her a small smile.

"Yeah, a bit. I'm really sorry you had to see that. God, I dread to think what I must look like after I've been crying for hours." Samantha forced out a laugh, hoping to make light of the situation.

Wardell brushed her hair back from her forehead and murmured, "You look lovely. Just like always." His eyes immediately widened as he seemed to realise what he'd just said, and he quickly dropped his hand. "Err, anyway, if you're better now, I should probably go home."

"Okay." Samantha's voice was quiet as she watched him try to avoid meeting her eyes. "Thank you for coming."

"It's no problem." He ran his hands through his hair nervously. "You probably shouldn't tell anyone that I was here though. It would sound a bit...inappropriate."

Her mouth felt suddenly parched and she had to clear her throat. "Okay. I won't."

As she watched Wardell start to stand up to leave, something suddenly overcame her and she reached out to wrap her hand around his arm.

"What's wrong?" he asked with a frown.

Samantha didn't answer with words.

Instead, she slowly leaned forwards and placed her lips on his.

Chapter Thirteen

There were a brief few seconds where Wardell didn't move; if anything, Samantha could have sworn she felt a slight pressure against her mouth, as if he was returning the kiss. But then he must have come to his senses because he quickly pulled away and stared at her in a stunned silence.

"Oh my god," Samantha muttered, automatically putting her hand over her mouth as if that could erase the stupid thing she'd just done. "I'm sorry. I shouldn't have done that."

She watched Wardell's throat move as he swallowed. "No, you shouldn't have." He looked away from her and got to his feet without her stopping him again. "I'm gonna go. I'll see you on Monday."

Samantha stayed frozen to her couch as he strode purposefully down the hallway and out of the front door.

If she had thought it was hard to shut her mind off earlier, it was *impossible* to do it once she got back in bed.

She just kept repeating the kiss over and over in her mind, berating herself for making a move on her therapist and no doubt making things permanently awkward between them in the future.

What had she been thinking?

She was never usually the sort of person to make the first move, so she didn't know what had made her do it that time. In that moment after he'd described her as lovely, she'd been convinced that he would return any kiss or gesture of affection from her; but she had been dead wrong.

It was humiliating to be rejected by such an attractive, older man; and the fact that before it had happened he'd been helping her through a mini breakdown just made the whole thing even worse.

She didn't know how she could face him again after what she'd done.

Should she quit her therapy?

But her mum and dad had already paid for at least another five sessions, she quickly realised. She wouldn't be able to cancel them without her parents finding out and asking what the issue was, and she obviously couldn't tell them the truth about *that*.

So what the hell was she supposed to do?

When Samantha finally fell asleep, she had one of those dreams that seemed to last for hours, but which really only probably lasted about ten minutes.

In it, she was stood on the side of the road again, watching the cars speed past and waiting for the perfect opportunity.

Finally, she saw one that seemed to stand out from the others, and she took a step off the pavement, as if in slow motion.

The car hit her and she was thrown in the air slightly before landing a couple of metres away.

In the dream, she felt all of the sensations that she remembered from the time. The blood trickling down her skin, the pain all over her body, and the rough gravel digging into her.

Her eyes stayed open this time, and she watched as Wardell rushed out of his car and ran over to her, sweeping her up into his arms as his worried gaze scanned her from head to toe.

"Oh my god. Oh shit. Are you okay?"

He took his phone out of his pocket to call an ambulance, but Samantha quickly knocked it out of his hand, causing him to stare at her in confusion.

"What's wrong?"

Samantha didn't speak. Instead, she wrapped her fingers tightly around the material of his shirt, pulled him towards her and covered his mouth with her own; smiling when he began to kiss her back just as hungrily as she was kissing him.

And then she woke up.

Chapter Fourteen

When Monday rolled around, Samantha was quite happy for her day at work to drag. Anything was better than having to go and see Wardell again after she'd kissed him and been rejected.

She wished she could just not go to their scheduled appointment, but knew her parents would find out if she skipped it, and didn't want to waste their money.

She still wasn't one hundred percent sure that she was actually going to go ahead with it until she walked through the doors, signed in with the usual receptionist, and went up the stairs to sit in the waiting room.

Thankfully, it was empty this time, so no one was there to stare at her whilst she sweated and tapped her foot up and down nervously.

She heard the door open but couldn't even bring herself to turn her head.

"Samantha? Come in."

She kept her gaze on the ground as she moved past him and went over to the familiar couch, purposely taking longer than was necessary to arrange her clothes neatly beneath her before she finally had to give in and meet his inquisitive gaze.

She waited for him to say something about Saturday night. Waited for him to put her straight by telling her how wrong it was and that it could never happen again or else he'd be forced to 'sack' her as his patient.

Instead, he didn't acknowledge it.

"I've spoken to your GP," he told her, seeming completely casual. "There should be a new prescription ready for you to pick up tomorrow."

"Oh. Thanks."

Wardell clicked on his pen. "So, let's begin with the usual questions. How was work today?"

"Err, it was fine," she said with a frown.

Although she was somewhat grateful that he was saving her from any embarrassment by not mentioning the kiss, she also found herself getting offended by how unaffected he obviously was.

As the session went on, Wardell asked her all of the usual questions and she answered them robotically, gradually getting more abrupt as it got later into their hour together.

If he noticed, he didn't pull her up about it, and instead went on acting like everything was normal.

"Okay, I think we'll leave it there for today," he said finally, shutting the screen of his laptop in what seemed to be a dismissal. "I'll see you on Friday."

"Yeah. Sure."

Samantha avoided looking at him as she stood up and moved towards the door, but she quickly came to a halt when she realised that she had yet again forgotten the bag that she'd left in his office after their appointment the previous Friday.

Turning to fetch it, she gasped as she found Wardell standing closely behind her, holding out the bag in question.

"Um, thanks," she said, taking it from him.

He grabbed her arm before she could move away again and then seemed to search her eyes for something. "Is everything okay? Are you mad at me about the other night?"

Samantha stiffened. "No."

"Yes you are," Wardell said with a sigh, letting go of her arm but continuing to stare intently at her. "Samantha, I'm sorry. But you must understand why I had to stop it?"

That piqued her interest. "What do you mean?

"You're my patient!" He sounded almost exasperated. "I'm not allowed to get involved with you like that. Do you realise how *wrong* that would be? I could lose my job."

Samantha understood every word he said, but her brain only fixated on one thing.

He hadn't said that he didn't *want* to kiss her.

As she scanned his features, she saw the conflict in his expression and her chest warmed as she suddenly realised what was really going on.

He liked her. He just didn't *want* to.

The surprising revelation was enough to boost her confidence and get her to drop the subject for the time being, until after she'd been able to think through everything properly and decide what to do next.

"Fine," she said, smiling brightly and confusing him with her sudden change in mood. "I'll see you on Friday, Doctor Briggs."

His eyes narrowed as he frowned. "You can still call me Wardell."

"Okay. Goodbye Wardell."

She smirked to herself as she felt his eyes on her back, watching her leave.

Chapter Fifteen

Samantha experienced a newfound happiness over the next couple of days.

As she thought over all of her interactions with Wardell, everything suddenly seemed to make sense.

He'd been the one to first touch her hand.

He'd invited himself to her flat, and then had chosen to hold her in his arms whilst she'd cried.

He'd stroked her hair back from her face and then given her a compliment.

She hadn't read too much into things at all.

He shared her feelings, she was sure of that.

She just didn't know what she was going to do about it.

Thinking about Wardell was a useful distraction though, and she found herself easily ignoring any intrusive thoughts that would usually keep her occupied for hours, because she wanted to focus on him instead, and daydream about what might happen when she next saw him.

She was usually a very passive person, and lived by the philosophy that whatever was meant to happen would happen, and she didn't go for things in the way that other people did; she just let them come to her.

When it came to her current situation, however, she wanted to change that.

She didn't know if it was her tablets working, or if her near suicide had given her a new lease of life, or if she was just desperate to find someone to make her happy and make her forget about all of her problems, but she was determined to not give up on the possibility of her and Wardell.

She wanted him.

And if he wasn't going to do anything about it, then she would have to do something herself.

Samantha put together a plan of action.

After work that Wednesday, she went to a bookshop in the city centre near where she worked and bought every self help book they had which claimed to teach a woman how to seduce a man.

By that point, she had already started to build up a story in her mind of her and Wardell having some kind of exciting forbidden romance where they had to sneak around and catch quick, heated moments together, so she was intent on making sure that happened.

She'd always had a tendency to obsess about things once she got an idea in her head, but with this new project she found herself even more invested than usual.

She read each book from cover to cover, highlighting certain sections which she thought were the most applicable to her, and writing notes for herself about how she could put each piece of advice into action.

Looking through her wardrobe, she planned an outfit to wear for that Friday's therapy session; one which would hopefully catch Wardell's eye and make him unable to turn away. Once that was sorted, she had nothing left to do but sit and wait.

Chapter Sixteen

On Friday afternoon, Samantha went into the toilets at work ten minutes before the end of the day to touch up her makeup and make sure that her clothes looked as nice as they had when she left her flat that morning.

She'd dressed in a white sleeveless blouse and a short grey skirt which she thought showed her figure off better than anything else she owned could. She'd paired the outfit with opaque black tights and a pair of small black heels which were the maximum height for what she could actually manage to walk in.

She'd put a full face of makeup on for the first time in what felt like years. Usually, she just wore a bit of lip gloss and mascara, and maybe added a thin streak of eyeliner if she had been crying and needed to try and disguise her puffy eyes. It was actually surprising to see just how much of a difference the face of makeup had made. She looked almost....decent. Not necessarily pretty, but she was confident that no one would describe her as ugly when she looked like that.

None of her work colleagues seemed to have noticed a difference in her appearance of course, but Samantha didn't let herself care.

It wasn't them she was trying to impress, after all.

Before she reached the building where her sessions took place, she quickly unbuttoned the top of her blouse, revealing just a bit of cleavage, but not so much where it seemed strange or obvious what she was doing.

The receptionist did a double take when she saw her, making Samantha smile to herself as she walked up the stairs and took a seat in the waiting room.

The man that she'd seen before was there again, and he too looked twice at her and smiled charmingly. "Hi."

"Err, hi," Samantha said, wanting to be polite but also not in the mood to talk to a random stranger.

He was still staring at her and smiling when Wardell opened the door a moment later.

Wardell's eyes widened slightly as he took her in, but Samantha pretended not to notice and just walked past him into his office, purposely brushing her body against his as she passed.

"Hey, how are you?" Wardell asked as he took a seat behind his desk.

"I'm fine. Work was fine too."

He chuckled at her preempting his next question. "Good. And how are your tablets? Did you start your new ones?"

"Yeah. I actually think I'm feeling a bit of an improvement. Or is it too soon for that?"

"No, it's not too soon. You've been on the lower dose tablets for a couple of weeks now, so chances are they've made a slight difference at least, but I'm still going to keep you on the higher dose tablets because I thought it would be likely you'd need them anyway with how severe your problems were." He made a note on his laptop before leaning back in his seat. "So, is there anything specific on your mind, or do you want to carry on with what you were telling me last week? About the bullies at your school?"

Samantha quickly searched her mind for a topic that would be both honest and suitable to discuss with her therapist, but would also help with her own plan for the day which was to make him uncomfortable and flustered.

"Actually, I was hoping we could start talking about something quite personal."

Wardell raised his eyebrows. "Okay. What is it?"

She forced herself to say the words, even though it meant being a lot bolder than she'd ever been before. "Well, I think I might be a bit obsessed with...sex."

Wardell's jaw dropped and she struggled to hide a self-satisfied smile.

Her statement was actually the truth and was something she'd questioned about herself for years so it seemed appropriate to talk about so she could try and find out if she was abnormal because of it.

Wardell cleared his throat. "Um, in what way? I thought you said you've not had many relationships?"

"Oh, no, I've not." Samantha waved her hand dismissively. "I just mean that I'm obsessed with reading about it and watching it. Is that weird?" She didn't actually give him a chance to answer before she added, "I mean, obviously I would like to have more sex. But I don't get many offers unfortunately."

"Well…" Wardell seemed at a loss for words. "It's probably your lack of experience with sex in real life that makes you enjoy experiencing it through other methods." He cleared his throat. "When you read these books, and watch things, do you…?"

"Get myself off?" Samantha finished for him. "Yeah. Most of the time."

His cheeks immediately turned pink. "That makes sense then. Some people seek pleasure by being promiscuous, you just do it differently."

"Oh. Fair enough." She forced out a natural sounding laugh. "Maybe I should mix it up a bit sometimes and find an actual guy to get me off."

Samantha watched his adam's apple move in his throat. "It probably wouldn't be appropriate for me to comment on that."

"Oh, sorry." She giggled and started twirling her hair around her finger; a tactic which every single one of her books had suggested. "Let's move on to something else then."

They spent the rest of the hour talking about which particular things she'd been worried about and checking that week.

Wardell seemed to never fully recover from their earlier conversation, but Samantha did her best to act as though she was completely unbothered by it.

"Any plans for the weekend?" he asked as he walked with her down the stairs.

"Err, I'll probably just try and keep my mind as busy as possible," she told him. "I don't want to have another meltdown like last weekend."

He gave her an awkward smile at the reminder. "That's a good idea. But remember, if you do have any issues, feel free to call me again."

"Oh, I definitely won't be doing that," Samantha said with a laugh, stroking her hand down his arm before she backed away from him towards the door. "See you next week."

Chapter Seventeen

Just wanted to check you're alright. Have you had any problems today?

The message took Samantha by surprise when it popped up on her phone screen, and she couldn't help the smile that immediately stretched across her face at knowing that Wardell had been thinking about her and had chosen to initiate contact outside of their scheduled appointments.

She didn't reply to the text for a couple of hours, hoping her delayed response would cause him to wonder what she was busy doing.

I'm fine. No issues, she wrote.

It was true.

She was still too wrapped up with Wardell and her plan for seducing him that she hadn't had time to worry about anything else.

Wardell replied almost immediately.

Good. I'm glad

Samantha frowned at the message. She'd been hoping for more from him, so was disappointed that he seemed to want to end their conversation so soon.

She wanted to quickly flick through her seduction books again to see if any of them gave suggestions about how to tease a guy through text, but she didn't want to risk Wardell walking away from his phone if she took too long so she quickly thought of something that could be enticing herself.

I'm touching myself right now and imagining you're here with me x

He didn't respond for almost ten minutes, and she stared at her screen the whole time, wondering if she had maybe gone too far and if instead of teasing him she had really just scared him away.

When a reply did finally come through, her stomach sank.

Samantha. Enough. Stop this. I mean it.

Shit.

Her plan had definitely backfired.

Samantha spent the whole of Sunday scrolling through the internet and flicking through her books to find a way to fix things with Wardell after she had messed up the day before.

Most of the things she read suggested that she ignore him when she next saw him. Obviously, she wouldn't be able to completely ignore him when she had to sit face to face with him in a reasonably small room for an hour, but she could act casual and aloof so that he would be confused by her sudden change in behaviour and would hopefully be thinking about her long after she left the appointment.

She bought herself a new outfit during her lunch break on Monday and quickly slipped into the form fitting, square necked black dress in the office toilets five minutes before the end of the day and then went to catch her bus.

"Doctor Briggs is overrunning with another patient," the receptionist told her when she arrived. "But just go up and wait for him and he hopefully shouldn't be too much longer."

Samantha took her usual seat in the corner and glanced at the clock every couple of minutes, willing Wardell and whoever he was with to hurry up.

She wondered if he could be purposely taking his time with the other patient as a way to try and avoid her, but then decided she was probably getting ahead of herself so told her weird brain to shut up.

His door finally opened and she turned to see a petite blonde girl coming out. She appeared to be in her early thirties, and didn't look anything like the sort of patient she would have expected to come across in a therapist's office. The broad smile on her face seemed strange, and the high pitched giggle that was coming out of her mouth confused Samantha.

Until she heard the deeper chuckle accompanying it as Wardell appeared in the doorframe behind her.

"Well, I'll see you next week Wardell," the girl said animatedly.

"Yeah, see you soon."

He hadn't even looked in Samantha's direction yet and she hated that. Not to mention the fact that he was letting the girl use his first name. Maybe she'd been stupid, but she had hoped that she might be his only patient that he allowed to do that.

The girl strutted out of the door, making sure to glance back over her shoulder to give Wardell one last alluring smile before it swung shut behind her.

It was only once she'd completely disappeared and they'd listened to the sound of her heels clicking down the stairs that Wardell finally looked at Samantha.

"Hey. Sorry I'm running late today. Are you ready to go in?"

She wanted to ask him about the girl. To find out what her name was, and to see if anything was going on between them, but she knew she couldn't.

She had a plan for the day, and she needed to stick to it so she gave him a small smile and acted completely unfazed as she stood up and said, "Yeah, I'm ready."

Chapter Eighteen

For once, Wardell didn't ask about her weekend, and she knew it was probably because he was worried she'd mention the message that she'd sent him about touching herself.

"How was work today?" he started with instead, resting his forearms on his desk and giving her a polite smile.

Samantha couldn't help but notice how different it was to the one he'd used on his previous patient.

"It was fine," she told him, choosing not to elaborate further.

"And how do you think you're getting on with your tablets?"

"Fine."

"Any improvements or worries?"

"No."

Wardell's forehead creased. "Okay. Have you thought about hurting yourself again recently?"

"No."

He struggled to hide his impatience. "Alright. Is there anything specific you'd like to talk about today?"

Worried that her aloofness was coming across as her just being bitter after his rejection, Samantha searched her mind for a real suggestion that wouldn't bring up any awkwardness between them.

"Um, how about we talk about the morning I decided to go and step in front of a car?"

Wardell looked surprised. "Really?"

"Yeah, we've never properly spoken about it before."

"I know. That's because I always assumed you weren't ready to. I didn't want to push you into it in case it made you uncomfortable."

Her chest warmed at his words. "Thank you. But I think I should be fine now."

Wardell nodded and slid his laptop and notepad away from him on the desk, giving her his full attention.

"Okay. So tell me what happened."

Samantha spoke non-stop for the next fourty five minutes; barely taking a breath or even pausing in her story each time she had to reach for a new tissue once her previous one was so wet that it was falling apart.

Wardell never interjected with any questions or comments about what she was telling him. He just let her speak, and she appreciated that.

"Then I stepped into the road and....your car hit me," she finished.

Neither of them spoke for a few minutes as Samantha dried the rest of her tears and Wardell either waited for her to say something else, or took some time to process everything she had revealed.

Finally, Samantha looked at the clock, seeing that their session was almost over. "Well, we should probably leave things there, right?"

Wardell blinked, breaking out of whatever thoughts he had been lost in. "Err, yeah. If you're sure you're done?"

She nodded and stood up. "Yep. That's everything."

"Okay, we'll pick this up on Friday then."

"Cool."

She turned towards the door but he stopped her.

"Samantha, are you sure you're okay?"

She gave him a bland smile. "Yeah. I'm fine. Bye Doctor Briggs."

"Wardell," he reminded her sternly, but she ignored him and left the room.

Chapter Nineteen

"We spoke to Wardell today," her dad said the next night when Samantha was in the middle of eating her dinner.

"Why?" she asked, internally starting to panic as she imagined a scenario where Wardell had rang her parents to tell them about her recent behaviour with him.

"We just wanted to ask how your therapy sessions were going," her mum explained. "You don't tell us much about them, so we were hoping he would instead."

"And did he?"

Her mum scowled. "No. He said he couldn't because of 'client confidentiality'." She rolled her eyes as if she found it ridiculous that parents were included in that rule. "He just said that things were going well and he's pleased with your progress."

Samantha felt herself growing irritated. "Good that's all I'd want him to tell you."

Her dad looked offended. "Why? We're the ones paying him to help you. So why shouldn't we get to know more about it?"

"Because it's none of your business!"

A half hour argument followed where her parents admonished her for apparently being ungrateful, and always being strange and secretive about her life.

Samantha began to cry, just like she always did whenever there was some kind of conflict, and her dad made her feel stupid about it until finally she left their house with tears streaming down her face and took a taxi back to her flat.

She was tearful for the rest of that week and felt as if she had no energy to do anything but lie on the couch and wait for her mood to get back to normal.

When she had tried to go to work on the Wednesday she couldn't concentrate on any of the tasks given to her and had ended up going into her supervisor's office with teary eyes and a choked voice, asking him to let her go home because she told him she wasn't feeling well.

She rang in sick for the next two days and even skipped her therapy session with Wardell on the Friday night, feeling in no mood to face him or carry out more of her stupid plan in her current condition.

He tried to call her once he obviously realised that she wasn't going to show up, and even sent a few messages asking where she was and if she was okay, but she ignored them all and put her phone on silent, wanting to hide away from him and the rest of the world.

"Please let me feel better tomorrow," she whispered later that night as she lay in her bed, staring up at the ceiling. "Please don't let me cry any more."

Chapter Twenty

A loud knocking on her front door woke Samantha up on Sunday morning.

The previous day had been just as bad as the three before it, but she'd hoped that having a lie in might improve her mood so wasn't happy to be forced out of bed before 10am.

Grumbling to herself, she wrapped her silk dressing gown around her body and went to find out who it was, hoping that she wouldn't find one of her nosey neighbours standing there wanting to gossip about someone else in the building.

However, as she opened the door, her face fell when she saw the last person she'd expected to be there.

Wardell.

"What are you doing here?" she asked him, hoping to not sound too rude.

He looked relieved for a brief moment but then shoved his hands deep into his pockets and shifted about awkwardly. "I was worried about you. You didn't turn up on Friday and you haven't returned any of my calls. I thought you might have done something."

For the first time, Samantha only just realised how her no show and silence could have been perceived after her past behaviour, and she immediately felt like an idiot for causing him to worry.

"I'm sorry," she said. "I didn't even think. I just...wasn't feeling up to it."

Wardell stared at her in disbelief. "You didn't feel up to it?"

"I-" She held her head in her hands for a moment and let out a heavy sigh. "I just really didn't want to be around anyone, and I can't stop crying and-" She broke off again and met his eyes. "Do you want to come in?"

He followed her inside and they sat down on her couch, turning their bodies to face each other whilst Wardell cast his worried glance over her face. "What's been going on Samantha?"

"I don't know. I've just been in a strange mood where I don't have any energy to do anything and I cry at the smallest things. I get like this sometimes. I just have to wait it out and it will go away eventually."

He gave her a sympathetic look. "You should have told me about it. I could have come here to do our session on Friday."

"Sorry, I didn't even think."

"It's okay." He tentatively reached out and placed a reassuring hand on her arm. "How do you feel today?"

"A bit better, maybe." She let out an exhausted sounding groan. "I just wish these tablets would start working properly."

"They will," he promised her, beginning to rub her arm. "You've only been on them for a few weeks. Give them a chance. It can take a couple of months for them to work sometimes."

"Great." She rolled her eyes but then smiled slightly. "Thanks for coming to check on me."

"It's okay." He suddenly seemed to realise that he was still touching her so quickly took his hand off her arm. "Erm, I should probably go home then."

"No, don't," Samantha said without thinking. She didn't want to risk him leaving and her spending the whole day crying again. "Do you want a drink or something? I'd actually like to talk to you a bit more, if you don't mind."

He seemed hesitant at first so she thought he was going to refuse; but then he smiled and said, "Sure. Can I have a coffee?"

"Of course." She made it for him and poured herself a glass of water before joining him back on the couch.

"Thanks." He took a sip. "So what did you want to talk about?"

Samantha quickly tried to search her mind, but couldn't think of anything to suggest as a topic. "Err, well, actually I just kind of wanted a bit of company. Is that okay?"

Wardell paused for a moment. "Um, yeah. That's fine."

They ended up watching television together and talking in a way that two friends would, instead of acting like patient and therapist.

She hadn't been planning on trying to seduce him whilst he was there, but when she felt his gaze on her and turned to find him staring at the hint of cleavage that was on show from where her dressing gown had loosened, she decided that it might be time for her to make another move.

She couldn't be bothered with subtlety anymore, however, and instead she chose to just go for it.

Without any warning, she turned and straddled Wardell's lap, pressing him back against the couch as he looked up at her with shock, before she slammed her mouth down on his.

Chapter Twenty One

Samantha couldn't believe her luck when Wardell actually started to kiss her back after only a couple of seconds of hesitation. Not only that, but he was moaning in the back of his throat as he moved his mouth greedily with hers whilst his warm hands stroked up and down her back.

She knew he'd eventually come to his senses and stop what was going on, so she tried to take full advantage of the situation and pulled back briefly to undo the tie on her dressing gown so that the material fell away from her body and revealed the skimpy pyjamas beneath.

"Touch me Wardell," she begged him in a breathy voice. "Please."

He stared at her chest with dark eyes, taking in the sight of her boobs practically spilling out of her vest top only a few inches away from his face; in a prime position for him to reach out and grab them, or to lean forwards and suck one of her nipples into his mouth through the material.

"Please Wardell," she said almost desperately.

She knew the instant reality hit him.

He screwed his eyes shut tightly and then gently pushed her off of his lap so that she was forced to move back to the seat beside him.

"I can't Samantha," he said in a strained voice.

"But-" She started to protest but he quickly waved his hand to cut her off and got to his feet.

"Forget this ever happened. *Please.*" he met her eyes seriously. "You can't tell anyone about this."

"I won't! We can keep it a secret!" She jumped up excitedly, remembering her idea about them engaging in a forbidden love affair. "Come on, Wardell. Kiss me again. It'll be fine."

He turned away, as if he didn't trust himself to not give in to her words. "No Samantha," he said forcefully, using a tone she'd never heard from him before.

"Fine." She felt herself begin to flush with humiliation and so said the first words that came into her head in an effort to act like she didn't care too much about his rejection. "I'll go and find somebody else to fuck."

He snapped his head back around to face her with a scowl. She expected him to berate her and to tell her that she was acting like a pathetic child, but instead he abruptly moved forwards and sealed their mouths together again, plunging his tongue between her lips as he began to lower them back down to the couch.

Chapter Twenty Two

Wardell covered her body with his, stretching out on top of her whilst he raised her arms above her head and threaded their fingers together.

She had never been kissed so passionately before, and she found herself practically squirming with need below him and letting out a small moan as her hardened nipples brushed against his firm chest.

Whilst he continued to kiss her, his hand reached into her shorts and found her clitoris, making her gasp against his mouth before she lifted her knees slightly to allow him better access as he began rubbing her furiously with just a single digit.

"Oh god," she moaned, not knowing how to control the feelings that were flooding her body. "That's, ugh, I can't-"

"Fuck Samantha," he groaned in a husky voice. "You're so wet. Is this what you're always like around me?"

She could only nod in response, but it was enough to spur him on further so that he soon slipped his finger into her opening whilst he used his thumb to continue to rub her.

Her orgasm hit her hard and she let out a loud moan whilst her body trembled from the pleasure. Wardell watched her intently throughout the whole thing, and once she'd finally settled down he bent his head and gave her a long, wet kiss.

"Do you want me inside you?" he murmured.

Samantha nodded eagerly, and then helped him pull down her shorts and his jeans just far enough to expose his thick erection and her dripping flesh before he finally slid into her in one smooth movement.

"Are you on the pill or anything?" he panted out between thrusts, pressing his forehead to hers as he moved within her expertly.

"Yeah. Don't worry." She'd never been more thankful for her painful, heavy periods that had made her be on the pill since she was seventeen. She didn't think she could have coped if he'd had to stop what he was doing right at that moment.

Sex had never felt so good.

As his movements became quicker and he began to groan more frequently, she knew he was already getting close and decided to help him along by cupping his backside and pushing him even more firmly into her whilst she wrapped her legs around him.

"Oh fuck Samantha." He moved his hand down to start rubbing her clitoris again and she soon found herself just as ready to explode as he was.

As she cried out once more, Wardell watched her with an enraptured expression for a moment before he finally let go himself and emptied inside her with a low moan.

They were silent for a long time; long after Samantha felt his deflated length slip out of her and rest against her thigh.

She wondered what he was thinking as he lay on top of her with his head pressed into the space between her shoulder and neck. His breathing was steady, and she didn't think he could be freaking out about what had happened because otherwise he would have climbed off her and probably run out of her flat without a backwards glance.

So what was going on in his head?

Finally, she became impatient and she started to stroke her fingers through his sweaty hair as she talked softly to him. "Wardell? Are you okay?"

He raised his head, staring down at her with an unreadable expression. "We shouldn't have done that."

Her stomach dropped, and she worried that she was going to do something stupid like burst into tears again.

"I know," she said quietly. "But I'm happy we did it. Aren't you?"

It seemed like an age before he nodded slowly and a reluctant smile spread across his face. "Yeah, I am."

Chapter Twenty Three

They spent the whole day together, wrapped in each other's arms under a blanket on her couch.

They didn't have sex again, but instead just watched television and got to know each other better.

She found out that his mum had walked out when he was two years old and he and his dad had never seen her again. It had been the reason why he'd decided to study psychology. He'd wanted to understand how a mother could abandon her child.

"Do you think you'll ever see her again?" Samantha asked softly.

He shook his head. "She died a few years ago. Her sister contacted my dad and told him. Apparently she'd suffered with depression for years and had turned to drugs because of it. That's what killed her."

"So is that why you decided to specialise in mental health?"

"Yeah. I just...wanted to help people realise there's another way out of things."

Samantha gazed at him in wonder, feeling as if he was some kind of hero. She definitely thought he was *her* hero.

"Would you think I was weird if I said I'm glad I walked in front of your car that day?"

He smiled at her and stroked his fingers through her hair. "No. I'm kind of glad you walked in front of my car too."

"I'll see you tomorrow then," Samantha said reluctantly when Wardell finally said he had to go home later that night.

"Yeah." He pressed a soft kiss against her mouth. "Listen, I know this probably goes without saying, but you know you can't tell anyone about us, don't you?"

She nodded, feeling excitement fizz in her stomach. "Yeah, I know."

When the door closed behind him, she immediately felt sad again and had to fight back tears. She knew it probably wasn't normal to have that reaction but she didn't allow herself to think too much into it.

You'll see him tomorrow, she reminded herself. *You only have to get through twenty two hours before you see him again at your appointment. That's nothing. And maybe you can even convince him to have sex in his office while you're there.*

The thought brightened her mood, and she took herself off to bed for an early night, mentally planning the outfit she would wear the next day, and what she would say to Wardell to get him to bend her over his desk and fuck her brains out.

Chapter Twenty Four

"You look nice," Wardell said with a grin as he let Samantha into his office the next afternoon.

"Thanks." She smoothed her hands down the pencil skirt and black blouse that she'd put on, pleased that she'd obviously made a good choice.

"So, let's get started." Wardell sat down in his chair and opened his laptop, making Samantha frown. "What's wrong?"

"You haven't kissed me," she said, hating how whiny her voice sounded.

"Err, well, I didn't think that would be appropriate. You're not here for that right now." She gave him a clueless look and he sighed. "Samantha, I'm still your therapist. I still need to help you. No matter what happens outside this office, I still think we should keep things professional when we're in here."

She knew she should have sat down, but for some reason she decided it was a good idea to keep pushing. "Don't you want to fuck me over your desk?" she asked in what she hoped was a seductive tone, slowly walking closer to him and leaning down far enough so that his eyes were level with her cleavage. "I've been imagining it all day."

Wardell cleared his throat and rolled his chair backwards to put some space between them. "Samantha, no. Sit down," he said, like a teacher scolding a student who was misbehaving. "If you can't act sensibly during our appointments, then nothing more can happen between us outside of them."

"Seriously?" She scowled and crossed her arms, hoping he would change his mind, but he just stared at her blankly. "Fine," she sighed eventually, before going to sit down on the couch whilst pouting like a child. "What do you want to talk about today?"

Wardell watched her for a moment, seeming concerned, but he didn't comment on her behaviour and just started the session.

At the end of the hour, Samantha tried her luck again.

"Now, will you fuck me?"

He gave her a warning glare. "No. Stop it."

"Oh, come on," she said with a laugh, approaching his desk and then rounding it so that she was standing right in front of where he was sitting. "Let's have a bit of fun. What's the problem with that? The session's over and we're the only people left in the building."

"No, Samantha. Go home. I'll call you or something."

She didn't like his answer. The only thing that had got her through the day was the thought of spending time with him and maybe doing something dirty, so she wasn't willing to leave until she'd found the distraction with him that she craved.

Suddenly having an idea, she slowly lowered herself to her knees and gazed up at Wardell through hooded eyes. "How about I just suck you off then? Would you like that?"

She was satisfied when she saw him swallow heavily, and it gave her the courage to reach out and curl her fingers around the bulge that was starting to grow between his legs. "Is this for me?" she asked as she started to stroke him through his trousers.

"Samantha." He said her name as a sort of protest, but didn't make any move to stop what she was doing, so she pulled his zip down and began to worm her hand into the elastic waistband of his underwear.

Wardell's hand quickly grasped her wrist. "No." From the tone of his voice, she could tell he was losing patience and knew she was likely to cause more trouble for herself if she tried to argue.

"Fine." She pulled back with a sigh and stood up. "I'll go then. But you said you'd call me, right?"

He didn't answer.

"Wardell?"

He looked away, avoiding her eyes, before speaking in an emotionless voice. "I don't think this is a good idea Samantha. I never should have given into you yesterday. It was wrong. This can't continue."

"Why?" Tears immediately filled her eyes as she internally berated herself for ruining things between them. "I'll act professional from now on. I promise."

"Samantha..." He shook his head, eyeing her warily. "I'm worried about you. I don't think you're in the right headspace to do this."

It was like a slap across the face. "What do you mean? Are you saying I'm crazy or something? Are you saying that I shouldn't have sex, just because I'm depressed?"

"No, it's not that-"

"Fuck off Wardell." She screamed it louder than she'd intended to, feeling suddenly out of control. "What's your excuse then? I didn't force you to have sex with me! If you're so worried about me, why did you fuck me on my couch yesterday?"

He looked ashamed. "I'm sorry. I *do* like you Samantha, but I should have known better. I should have stopped it sooner." He ran his hand through his hair in frustration. "What I did...people would see it as me taking advantage of you."

"Taking *advantage* of me?" She scoffed. "I'm not a child! I knew exactly what I was doing. I fucking planned it!"

"What?"

"Nothing." She shook her head, wishing she could take back her words.

He rose to his feet so that they were stood face to face, only inches apart. "What did you mean, you *planned* it?"

"I bought some books," she told him, hoping she could downplay how weird it probably sounded. "Books about how to seduce someone. I wanted to seduce *you*, but it didn't really go to plan, so when you turned up at my flat yesterday I decided to just go for it, and it worked."

Wardell was speechless for a few moments. His mouth opened and closed a few times as if he was trying to find the right words.

Finally, he turned away and went to flip through his diary on his desk. "I think we need to discuss this more. I can stay late tomorrow night. Would you be free to come for an extra session at 7pm?"

Samantha looked between him and his diary with disgust. She was sick of him patronising her and trying to make her feel like some kind of freak instead of just a woman who fancied a guy and who had decided to go after what she wanted for once.

There was nothing more to it than that.

"Fuck you Wardell," she said through a clenched jaw. "I don't want to see you ever again. I don't want you to be my therapist anymore. I'm gonna tell my mum and dad to cancel the sessions and get their money back."

"Samantha, I'm trying to help."

The tone of voice he used angered her further. He spoke to her as if she was a baby or some kind of cornered animal.

Before she even properly realised what she was about to do, her arm swung out and she thumped him in the jaw. Not as hard as she would have liked, but enough to knock his head back.

"Oh my god," she whispered, staring at him in horror as she slowly realised what she'd just done. "I'm sorry."

"It's okay," he said, surprising her, but she noticed that he was still speaking in that same patronising voice. "Just sit down. Let's talk a bit more."

"No." She abruptly turned away from him and went to fetch her bag from the couch. "I need to go home. I need to..." she trailed off as she left the room.

As she stumbled down the stairs and out through the glass front doors, she wasn't aware of anything but the blood pulsing in her ears and the tears dripping down her cheeks.

What's happening to me? She thought as she stood on the pavement, seeing the bright lights from cars flashing by. *I need to stop this before I get any worse.*

Her feet began to move forward of their own volition, taking her nearer to the edge of the road and nearer to the possibility of death.

Surely I wouldn't fail twice, she thought as she sized up the next car that was going to pass.

A hand suddenly wrapped around the top of her arm and pulled her backwards until she was leaning against a hard chest.

Wardell's chest.

"Don't do it," he panted softly, sounding out of breath. "I'm here. I can help you. You just have to let me."

Samantha started sobbing. "But it's so *hard*."

"I know." He wrapped his arms around her and leaned his cheek against the top of her head. "I know it is, baby."

Chapter Twenty Five

Wardell took her back up to his office and spent another hour trying to calm her down enough so that he felt safe sending her home by herself.

"Are you sure you don't want me to call your mum and dad?" he asked her, as they stood waiting for the taxi he'd ordered to arrive. "Or why don't you go and stay with them tonight?"

Samantha shook her head. "I'll be fine," she assured him. "I need to be alone for a while."

"Okay." He still didn't seem sure. "Well, let me know when you get in, and I'll text you later to check that you're alright."

She gave him an awkward smile, still not knowing how to act around him after everything that had happened between them. "Thanks."

The taxi pulled up a minute later and Wardell opened the door for her to climb inside. "So, I'll see you for our appointment tomorrow?"

Samantha stared up at him, feeling both grateful and embarrassed. "Yeah. I'll see you tomorrow Wardell."

He smiled at hearing his first name and then shut the door, letting the taxi drive her off into the night, whilst Samantha stared out of the window feeling numb.

The next morning, Samantha's mind felt slightly clearer and she was able to fully appreciate just how much of a mess she'd made of her life.

She almost couldn't bear the thought of having to go to work and pretending to be normal when the night before she'd been stood on the side of a road contemplating suicide again, but she knew that staying in on her own all day would just give her too much time to think so she forced herself out of bed and into the shower before dressing in something smart yet comfortable.

She wasn't in the mood to make too much of an effort, and after her confrontation with Wardell she knew there would be no point in trying to continue with her plan of seduction.

Besides, he'd made it clear that he wouldn't let anything else happen between them, especially not when she was only hanging on to her sanity by a thread, so she decided that she wasn't going to embarrass herself further by trying to change his mind.

A small voice in the back of her brain tried to tell her that there could be a chance of something happening in the future if she got herself sorted out, but she did her best to ignore it, knowing that it would be stupid to get her hopes up.

It shouldn't be a priority at the moment, anyway, she told herself. *Just concentrate on getting yourself better. That's all that matters for now.*

The work day thankfully passed quickly, and then Samantha had an hour to kill before her therapy appointment so she decided to go to a fast food restaurant near Wardell's office.

She was almost surprised that he hadn't tried to contact her to double check that she was definitely coming, or just to see how she was, but she told herself not to read into it too much because he was probably busy with other things.

At quarter to seven, she threw her rubbish away and walked over to the office, giving the receptionist an embarrassed smile when she saw how shocked the woman seemed to be to find her there two days in a row.

Wardell was just seeing his previous patient out when she arrived in the waiting room, and they both watched the older man disappear before turning to one another.

"How are you feeling?" Wardell asked quietly.

Samantha shrugged. "Better." She looked around nervously. "Do you usually do appointments this late?"

"Sometimes. When I think someone urgently needs help."

She met his serious gaze and decided to get something off her chest before they started.

"I'm sorry about last night," she told him. "I'm sorry for hitting you, and for behaving how I did. You have no idea how embarrassed I am about it all, and about all the other things I've done recently. But I want you to know I'm not going to do anything like that again. I promise. So, do you think we can have a fresh start?"

Wardell frowned slightly at first, but then she watched his broad chest expand and deflate with a heavy breath as he seemed to resolve something inside himself.

"Yeah Samantha. A fresh start it is."

Chapter Twenty Six

Two Months Later

Samantha blinked open her eyes and waited a few moments for the thoughts to start crowding in.

Nothing came.

She smiled giddily to herself as she climbed out of bed; the fourth day in a row where she had been able to rise straight after waking, without having to straighten a few things in her mind first.

The last couple of months had been some of the hardest in her life.

After her meltdown and other erratic behaviour with Wardell, he'd realised that her tablets obviously weren't working, and were even causing something called 'hypersexual behaviour', so he had decided to wean her off them and put her on some new ones.

The weaning procedure had been awful. For almost two weeks she'd had shaking hands and she'd had to fight off more suicidal thoughts. Thankfully, Wardell had been there to help her through it until she'd finally been able to start the new antidepressants which had worked much better.

After only a couple of weeks, she'd started to notice an improvement, and things had gradually got better from there until a few days ago she'd finally been able to wake up with a clear mind.

Her problems were still nowhere near being fully resolved, but they were a lot more manageable and she had started to almost feel like a normal person again, instead of letting her mental health problems rule her entire life.

She'd found work to be a lot more tolerable since her anxiety had started to lessen. She still doubted that she would ever make friends with her colleagues, but the tasks she was given were a lot easier when her OCD wasn't making her check everything about twenty times before she trusted that she'd actually done it right.

After she left the office that Friday evening, she felt like there was almost a spring in her step as she boarded the bus and rode to her therapy appointment. She couldn't wait to tell Wardell the good news about her improvement over the past few days.

Things between them had been great since he'd saved her from a second suicide attempt. They'd kept things strictly professional and hadn't mentioned any of the kisses they'd shared or the sex on Samantha's couch. Instead they'd abided by an unspoken agreement where they both pretended that the other stuff had never happened and that they'd only ever been friends.

There'd been a few times where Samantha had wondered if Wardell still had an interest in her, but she'd been too scared to mention it in case he rejected her or thought she was being promiscuous again.

If it's meant to be, it'll be, she'd told herself, putting her feelings for him to the back of her mind and deciding to just concentrate on getting better instead.

"Samantha." Wardell grinned down at her after opening his office door. "Come in."

They exchanged the usual pleasantries and then she told him about her latest news.

"I got out of bed straight away for the last four mornings," she said excitedly, knowing he would appreciate just how big of a deal that was.

"Really?" He raised his eyebrows and smiled. "That's great!" He typed a few notes into his laptop. "And what about work? Any troubles there?"

They spent the next hour drawing up a list of the things that Samantha thought she still needed to improve on so that Wardell would be able to plan their next few sessions.

"Over the weekend I'd also like you to start thinking about some life goals for yourself," he told her as she was getting ready to leave.

"Life goals?"

"Yeah. Now that you've started to get back on track, I think it would be good to think of other things you'd like to achieve so we can start working on them."

"Oh, okay." She was pleased to hear that they would be moving on to what was obviously the next stage of therapy. "So, you think I'm ready for that?"

"Of course." His dimple appeared. "You're like a different person compared to the girl I met a few months ago."

"Is that a bad thing?" Samantha asked teasingly; only realising once the words were out of her mouth that her question could be interpreted as flirting.

Wardell eyed her silently for a moment, and she thought she detected a slight blush on his cheeks.

"No," he murmured. "It's a good thing."

Chapter Twenty Seven

"We're thinking about cancelling your therapy sessions," Samantha's mum announced during lunch on Sunday.

She almost dropped her fork in surprise. "Why?"

"Well, you said you're feeling better now, didn't you?"

"Yeah..." Samantha said slowly. "But I'm not healed or anything. I still struggle with things."

"Yes, but you probably struggle with things in a much less serious way now, right?"

"Um."

"What your mum means," her dad interjected. "Is that these therapy sessions were only supposed to help you through your suicidal stage. And now that you've got past it and your tablets are working, we think it's a good idea for you to just go on the hospital waiting list for free therapy there."

"Oh. Right. Yeah."

Samantha knew she couldn't really argue because her parents had been generous enough by paying for private sessions for three months, but she hated the idea of having to stop going because it would mean that she would have no excuse to see Wardell anymore.

"That's fine. You can cancel them."

"Great," her mum beamed. "Well, we've paid up until the end of next week so you can go to two more and then you'll be finished. Do you want to tell Wardell, or should we call him?"

Samantha imagined the man in question, wondering if he would be disappointed to lose her as a patient and a sort of friend.

After everything that they'd shared together, it seemed implausible to think that they would soon have no reason to stay in contact anymore, and Samantha briefly considered whether she should make another move.

No, she thought, dismissing the idea immediately.

She couldn't risk embarrassing herself again.

If anything else was going to happen between her and Wardell, he was going to have to initiate it.

Samantha arrived at her appointment slightly early the next day, and took a seat in the waiting room as she tried to figure out how she would explain to Wardell why her sessions with him were suddenly being cancelled.

She didn't want him to think it had been her choice in any way, but also didn't want her parents to come across as selfish or unsympathetic to her problems by telling him the truth.

Her head turned curiously when she heard a high pitched giggle coming from inside Wardell's office, and as the door opened and the flirty blonde girl she'd seen once before stepped into the waiting room, her face froze.

The woman flipped her long hair back over her shoulders as she turned to Wardell with a coy smile. "Thanks for listening to me today. It was a big help."

"No problem," Wardell said politely. Samantha examined him closely, trying to see if there were any hidden emotions behind his eyes as he stared at his patient, but was relieved to find nothing of concern.

The blonde girl attempted to make more conversation with him about random things that were nothing to do with therapy, so Wardell eventually had to dismiss her quite abruptly.

"Sorry, I've got another patient," he said, interrupting her in mid sentence as he gestured towards where Samantha was sitting watching them. "I'll see you next week, Jersey."

"Oh." She didn't look happy. "Fine then. See you next week, Wardell."

She turned and flounced away, being sure to give Samantha a scathing look as she did so, as if she'd done something wrong by daring to have an appointment with her therapist.

"Sorry about that," Wardell said with an awkward smile before gesturing towards his open door. "Come in."

Once they were both situated in their usual seats, Samantha quickly started to speak before he had a chance to start the session properly.

"Err, Wardell, I've got something to tell you."

He frowned. "Okay. What is it?"

"Um, well, I'm quitting therapy."

His mouth opened and closed a couple of times before he managed to finally get some words out. "Why would you want to do that?"

Samantha shrugged, trying her best to seem casual and as if she didn't see it as a big deal. "I just don't think I need it anymore. I mean, you said yourself how much better you think I am. So I think I can handle things on my own from now on."

Wardell didn't look convinced and he eyed her sceptically until she finally gave in with a sigh.

"Okay, fine. My mum and dad want me to quit. They want me to just go on the waiting list for free therapy at the hospital."

"But why? Do they have a problem with me or something?"

"No!" she said quickly. "They just said that it's getting expensive so they can't really afford it anymore."

"Oh." His eyes quickly flickered around the room as if he was trying to find a solution to the problem. "Well, that shouldn't mean you have to quit."

"What?"

He shrugged. "I could give you the sessions for free. We've known each other for a few months now, so I'd hate to give up on you when you're just starting to get back to normal."

"You'd really do that?"

"Of course. And that way, we wouldn't have to stick to strict time limits, and you wouldn't even have to come here if you didn't want to. We could do the sessions at your flat."

Wardell seemed suddenly nervous and Samantha wondered if there was maybe more to what he had just suggested, although she told herself to not get her hopes up.

"Alright," she said quietly. "If you really wouldn't mind doing that, then it would be great. Thank you."

"No problem."

They watched each other intently, and Samantha felt her dormant attraction for him begin to manifest itself again.

She felt like something was happening, but she just needed him to be the first one to confirm it.

He didn't.

Instead, he turned back to his laptop as if the last few moments hadn't happened; immediately reverting back into his therapist persona.

"So, did you come up with any life goals?"

Chapter Twenty Eight

"Okay, we'll leave it there for today." Wardell said as he closed his laptop and began to pack away the items on his desk.

Samantha didn't move from her seat.

She'd spent their whole hour together thinking over the moment they'd shared, and comparing the way he'd looked at her with the way he'd looked at Jersey.

"Are you okay?" Wardell asked, when he saw that she was still sitting on the couch.

"Yeah." She shifted about a bit. "I was just wondering if there's something going on between you and that Jersey girl?"

He seemed almost angered by the question, and she wished she'd never bothered to voice it. "No. What makes you think that?"

"I don't know." She tried to avoid his eyes. "I've just seen her flirting with you a few times so I thought…." She trailed off when she saw how offended he looked.

"She's my *patient*, Samantha," he reminded her, as if that was enough of an answer.

"Yeah, but....that didn't exactly stop you with *me*, did it?"

It came out like an accusation, instead of as a hint to get him to compliment her in some way or admit his feelings like she'd intended to get him to do.

Wardell's face hardened in a way she'd never seen before; not even when she was acting her worst around him. "Is that really what you think of me?" he asked in a low voice. "That I take advantage of my female patients and go around fucking them all?"

Samantha almost flinched at the word. "No, I didn't mean it like that. I'm sorry."

He didn't give her a chance to explain. "I think you should leave. I'll see you on Friday."

"No, Wardell-"

He stormed out of the room before she could finish the sentence.

Chapter Twenty Nine

Wardell ignored all her messages that week, and was still in a mood when she arrived for their final paid session together on Friday.

Samantha worried that he'd revoke his offer to keep helping her unless she made things right between them before the end of that hour, and so she tried her best to act normal and friendly with him, and to try and engage him in conversation that wasn't just about her mental health.

But none of it worked.

He seemed determined to stay angry with her, and he barely met her eyes for the whole hour that she was sat in front of him.

Eventually, she lost patience. "What's wrong with you?"

Wardell snapped his head up, wearing a blank expression. "Nothing."

"You're still mad at me about what I said the other day."

"No I'm not."

"Yes you *are*." It was like they were two children having an argument. "I told you I was sorry though. I didn't mean for it to sound as bad as it did."

Wardell scoffed. "Really? So you didn't intend to make me feel like some kind of predator? It wasn't you getting payback for how I rejected you?"

Samantha was completely taken aback. "No! Of course it wasn't!"

"Sure." He looked away again, winding her up further, and making her automatically rise to her feet and move over to his desk so that she could tip his chin up herself.

"It wasn't payback," she told him, enunciating each word. "It was another one of my pathetic attempts to try and get you to tell me that you still like me."

Wardell stared at her, looking flushed. "Really?"

"Yeah." She couldn't resist adding, "You idiot."

He smirked, gazing at her warmly before his expression suddenly turned serious again as she watched his throat move with a gulp. "Samantha, I should probably tell you something."

This is it, she thought. *He's finally going to admit his feelings, and we're finally going to be together.*

"What is it?"

He ran his fingers through his hair and pulled at the roots roughly, making her wonder why he seemed to be having such a hard time getting the words out.

"I *did* sleep with Jersey," he admitted quietly, shocking her to the core, and making her dreams of them together disappear in an instant.

"What?" She couldn't quite believe what she'd just heard.

"It was a long time ago," he said desperately, standing up and reaching for her, but she quickly stepped back. " It was way before I met you, and it was only once! It didn't mean anything. We were both just drunk. But it was unprofessional, and I've hated myself for it ever since. She's tried to get me to do it again and I always refuse, but I can't risk getting rid of her as a patient in case she reports me and I lose my job."

Samantha struggled to take everything in. "But, you said you hadn't. And then you got *angry* with me."

"I know," he sighed, looking at her pitifully. "I was ashamed. And what you said hit a nerve." He tried reaching for her again but put his arm down when she automatically flinched. "I know it must look bad," he said, imploring her with his eyes. "But I promise I wasn't just using you. I *do* really like you, Samantha. I mean, believe me, I've questioned myself about what kind of person it makes me if I've slept with two patients, but I swear I have real feelings for you. What we have together is nothing like that night I spent with Jersey. Do you believe me?"

She stared at him wordlessly, not knowing what to believe.

He suddenly seemed like a completely different person to the one he was a few minutes ago, and she couldn't help but feel uncomfortable in his presence.

"I need to go," she said quietly, backing away from him slowly, as if he would lunge at her if she moved too fast.

"Samantha..." He reached his hand out once more. "I'm sorry. Please let me explain more."

"No," she said firmly, surprising both of them with the fierceness of her tone.

With no more words needed, she turned and fled the room.

She had no intention of seeing that office or its occupant ever again.

Chapter Thirty

Samantha had barely gotten a foot through her front door when she heard her phone beep with a message.

Rolling her eyes, she pulled the phone out of her pocket and huffed when she saw Wardell's name on the screen.

Samantha, I'm sorry. Please don't hate me. That night with Jersey happened nearly three years ago! It meant nothing.

She stabbed the screen angrily as she typed a reply.

I don't care. It doesn't change anything. Just leave me alone.

How can you say it doesn't change anything?! It's not like I've been having some kind of sordid relationship with her! It was one night of stupidity.

Samantha scowled to herself.

She's your patient! Do you seriously expect me to believe that it's a coincidence that you've slept with two of your patients?

Stop acting as if I'm some kind of groomer! I've been a therapist for over ten years now. One mistake with one patient during that whole time doesn't make me a pervert.

Samantha could see his point, but she still felt uncomfortable about the whole thing.

Two patients, she reminded him.

You're different. What happened with you wasn't a mistake. I have real feelings for you. I don't have any for Jersey.

She automatically smiled when she read those words, but told herself to be cautious and to get all the details before she made a decision about how she felt.

So what exactly happened with Jersey?

It took a while before her phone beeped with his response, but when she saw the paragraph he'd written she understood why.

I was out with my friends one night and bumped into her in a bar. I'd already had a few drinks by that point, and she kept buying me more. It was stupid of me to not realise what she was doing, and it was unprofessional of me to get drunk with her, but I did and then I ended up going home with her. When I woke up the next morning I told her it was a mistake and that it could never happen again. She wasn't happy, but I've always made sure to keep her at arms length. Nothing has happened since then. I promise.

How long has she been your patient in total?

About 5 years. She has a lot of issues....

The cryptic statement piqued her interest, but she knew he wouldn't tell her any more.

Whilst she tried to think of what to say next, another message came through from Wardell.

Samantha, believe me, my relationship with you is completely different. It has been since the first day I met you. Since I held you in my arms whilst I waited for the ambulance. I've always felt a connection to you, and what happened between us on your couch just made my feelings even stronger. I promised myself afterwards that I'd leave you alone until you got properly better, but now that you've improved so much, and now that you're no longer my patient I was hoping you might finally let me take you out. I told you about Jersey because I wanted to be honest. But I hate that I've ruined everything. Please forgive me. Or at least give me a chance to try and prove to you that I'm serious about wanting to start something with you.

Samantha read back through the whole conversation a couple of times, but finally decided that she believed every word he'd said.

She had no more questions or accusations left for him to clear up, and therefore had no reason to want to keep on rejecting him.

Still, she didn't want to make it too easy because she didn't want to risk looking like a pushover and setting a precedent for the future.

Okay. I'll give you another chance. But I don't want to rush straight back to the point we were at two months ago. I want to go slow.

His reply that time was immediate.

That's fine by me :) Thank you x

I'll see you at my flat on Monday for therapy then.

I was hoping I could take you out tomorrow night or something? X

Her heart urged her to accept his invitation but she stayed resolute.

Maybe next weekend. For now, I'll just see you on Monday.

Chapter Thirty One

Wardell was already there waiting outside her door when Samantha got home from work the following Monday.

"Oh," she said, surprised to see him, and embarrassed about the state she must be in after getting caught in a sudden downpour. "You're early."

"Yeah." He eyed her with amusement. "Is it raining?"

Samantha just gave him a look, making him laugh, and then she unlocked her door and led him inside.

"Err, you can sit down," she told him, gesturing towards the couch. "I'm gonna go and change into something dry."

She turned to glance over her shoulder at him as she walked towards her bedroom, and saw him staring down at the couch, seemingly lost in a memory.

She knew without having to ask that he must have been thinking of the last time he'd sat there. The time when he'd been pounding into her, making her orgasm harder than she ever had before.

He looked up suddenly and caught her watching him.

"Sorry," Samantha said, feeling her face flush. "I'll be out in a minute." She spun away again after giving him a tentative smile, feeling his hot gaze on her back as she disappeared into her room.

Once she was comfy in some fresh pyjamas, she went back out and joined him, seeing that he'd set up a notepad on the coffee table in front of him.

"Am I allowed to sit on the couch with you, or should I sit somewhere else so that it feels more like a real appointment?" she joked.

Wardell rolled his eyes. "Sit on the couch." He twisted around to face her once she was settled. "Ready?"

Things felt so different between them compared to the last time they'd been together. For one, the setting of her flat and knowing there was no chance of them being interrupted made it seem a lot more intimate, and after their conversation on Friday, Samantha wasn't really sure how to act around him.

She gave him a nervous smile. "Err, I came up with a few more goals to add to my list."

"Oh yeah?" He seemed pleased, almost as if he was proud of her. "What are they?"

"I think I'd like to write some kind of self help book one day. About overcoming suicidal thoughts and depression and stuff. I mean, it's probably been done before, but I think I'd still like to write it, even if the only person who ever reads it is me."

Wardell grinned at her. "I'd read it too. I'm assuming you'd mention me in it?"

Samantha giggled. "Only a little bit. You'll just be the shadow through the windscreen as the car screeches towards me."

She was pleased that she'd reached a point where she could joke about how bad she'd been. Since the beginning, there'd always been something about Wardell's presence that had made her feel calm and comfortable, but as she'd got to know him more she'd realised that it wasn't just a therapist thing. It was a *Wardell* thing.

He'd quickly become her best friend, and the person she felt the closest to in the world.

And now, she was sure he was going to become more than that.

"I think that's a really good idea," he told her, breaking her out of her thoughts. "I could even help you with it, if you wanted? I could tell you the technical terms for things and speak about the psychology behind it all."

Samantha barely paid him any attention.

She had the sudden urge to throw herself at him. Not because she was being hypersexual or was just desperate for a distraction, but because she had realised how much she wanted him, and how desperate she was to have him inside of her again.

Right then and there.

Wardell broke off mid sentence as he noticed whatever expression was on her face. His eyes darkened as they penetrated into her, watching and waiting for whatever she was about to do next.

The air around them felt heavy with anticipation, and Samantha licked her dry lips as she silently willed him to lean forwards and kiss her first for once.

He must have read her mind because in the next second he was suddenly pouncing on her, capturing her lips with his own and sliding his tongue into her mouth whilst their hands clawed at each other's bodies like a pair of animals.

Samantha broke away briefly, intending to start pulling Wardell's t-shirt off in a wordless indication as to what she wanted, but he quickly caught her wrists.

"What's wrong?" she asked breathlessly.

He stared at her with heated eyes and shook his head. "Nothing. I just don't want to have a quick fuck on the couch again." He quirked an eyebrow suggestively. "Bedroom?"

Chapter Thirty Two

His body came down on top of hers, pressing her into the mattress as he attached their lips again and continued on from where they'd left things in the living room.

"Are you sure you want this?" Wardell murmured against her mouth as he hands moved to grip the bottom of her pyjama vest.

Samantha nodded enthusiastically and reached to undo the button on his jeans whilst he pulled her vest over her head. The rest of their clothes quickly followed until they were soon both completely naked and Samantha could feel Wardell's hard length throbbing between her thighs.

When she went to wrap her fingers around it to guide him inside of her, he stopped her again.

"What's wrong now?" she asked, hearing the impatience in her own tone.

Wardell laughed. "Nothing. I just want to do something for you first before we get to that."

"Oh," Samantha murmured, letting her hand fall. She held her breath as he moved down the bed, positioning himself perfectly in order to access the sensitive flesh at her core.

When his tongue touched her for the first time, she let out a loud gasp and immediately arched her back off of the mattress.

"Do you like that?" Wardell asked huskily as he looked up at her from beneath heavy eyelids.

Samantha didn't answer with words and instead just wrapped both her hands through his hair and held his head still as she lifted her pelvis, urging him to carry on with what he had started.

She felt him smile against her, but he did what she wanted and began to lick and suck her again, gradually building up the pressure of his mouth and tongue until she was practically vibrating with need as she neared her climax.

Just as she thought he was about to take her over the edge, he abruptly moved his head away and crawled back up her body with a smirk on his face.

Samantha frowned at him dazedly, wondering why he'd stopped, but he prevented her from saying any words by claiming her mouth again, letting her taste herself on his tongue in a way which was strangely erotic.

"I want to make you come with my dick," he told her. She felt him nudging at her entrance. "Do you want that?"

Her fingers dug into his hips, trying to pull him down into her. "Do it."

"Do what?" he asked teasingly.

Samantha almost groaned in frustration. "Fuck me!"

She hadn't meant to say it so loudly, but Wardell seemed to enjoy hearing it, and he soon plunged inside her body without any more hesitation.

Samantha had never experienced having sex without a condom before him, and she was amazed by just how much better it was; although she thought that a big reason for that was also probably because of who she was doing it with.

"Fuck." Wardell had an intense look of concentration as he watched the place where their bodies were joined, and he glanced up every now and again to confirm that she was enjoying what he was doing. "This feels fucking amazing."

"I know," Samantha said breathlessly, struggling to keep her eyes open as he sped up his pace.

"Hold on to the headboard," he told her.

She followed his command without question, trusting that whatever he was preparing to do would be something she enjoyed.

Once she had a firm grip on the bars, Wardell slipped out of her and pulled on her legs so that she was stretched out to full length. Moving to a kneeling position, he lifted her hips into the air and then slammed back into her.

"Oh god," Samantha moaned. She automatically bent her knees a bit and raised them towards her chin to give him a better angle, and then they both groaned together as he slid even further into her, until she could feel his heavy balls slapping against her backside.

"Fuck Samantha. Fuck. Fuck."

Her orgasm hit her without warning, shattering throughout her body whilst she shook with pleasure.

"Yes," he hissed through his teeth. "That's it baby. Clench around me."

As she continued to ride the waves of her climax, she had a vague thought about how strange it was to see such a different side to her therapist, but it quickly left her mind when she felt him suddenly still his movements and then release inside of her.

"Oh, oh, oh fuck yeah!"

He collapsed on top of her, and she slowly let go of the bars of her headboard to wrap her arms around his back instead.

"Mmm," he hummed against her throat as she stroked her fingers over his sweaty skin. "That's nice."

"Which bit?"

"All of it. The sex, the coming, the cuddling, and the stroking of my back part."

Samantha giggled and couldn't resist pressing a soft kiss against the top of his head. "Yeah. It is nice."

Wardell lifted up slightly and gazed at her with a serious, thoughtful expression. "I should probably take you on a real date now. I mean, if you want to?"

She almost squealed in excitement. "Of course I want to."

"Great."

He leaned down to kiss her again.

Chapter Thirty Three

They saw each other every night that week and had sex many more times, but Wardell never slept over because he said he only wanted to do that once they'd had their first date which he had arranged for that Saturday night.

"You can stay at my house afterwards," he suggested. "You've never been there before, so it will feel more special."

"Plus, I'm guessing the house of a therapist is a lot nicer than the tiny flat of an office worker," she joked.

"True."

Wardell still made sure to sit down and have a therapy session with her after she'd got in from work on the Friday night, saying that he didn't want to risk her going backwards with her progress just because they were now in a relationship.

"This is weird," Samantha said with a nervous giggle as they sat opposite each other on her couch. "I don't know how to talk to you anymore."

"What do you mean?" Wardell frowned. "You never usually have a problem, and if anything I'd think it would be even easier to talk to me now."

"Yeah, I know." Samantha sighed. "But, I don't know, I'm more self-conscious now. I don't want to risk putting you off me by telling you about the weird stuff that goes on in my mind."

Wardell squeezed her hand reassuringly. "You won't put me off you. That's not possible."

"Really?"

He gave her a teasing grin. "If I was going to get put off you, don't you think it would have been when you were rolling across my car bonnet, or when you turned into a sexual deviant, or when you *punched* me?"

Samantha blushed at the memory of everything she'd done since she first encountered him. "Yeah, I suppose you're right." She released a long breath and met his eyes again. "Okay then, what should we talk about first, Doctor Briggs?"

Wardell laughed but started the session.

Their date was the next day, and Samantha spent most of the afternoon getting ready for it. She plucked her eyebrows, applied body cream to every inch of her skin and took twice as long on her makeup compared to usual so that she felt as perfect as possible when she slipped her new dress over her head ten minutes before Wardell was due to pick her up.

She'd bought a teal green maxi dress which she thought went well with her eyes, and paired it with gold bangles on either arm and large gold hoops in her ears.

As she examined her reflection in the mirror, she was surprisingly pleased with what she saw, and she went to answer the door with a smile on her face once her date arrived.

"Wow," Wardell said, running his gaze down her body. "You look beautiful."

"Thanks."

"Are you ready to go?"

She curled her fingers between his.

Chapter Thirty Four

Wardell took her to a bar which also had an adults only arcade within it.

She hadn't even known it existed but she fell in love with the place as soon as she walked inside and looked around at all of the retro arcade machines, air hockey tables and even bumper cars that were there.

A bar on the far left hand side of the building was serving drinks, and another at the opposite end was serving different types of chicken and chips in baskets.

"This is cool," Samantha said with a grin. "Have you been here before?"

"No, I've just heard a lot about it." Wardell looked slightly uncomfortable all of a sudden. "But, now that I'm here, I think I might be a bit too old."

Samantha scoffed. "What do you mean?"

"I'm about ten years older than everyone else," he pointed out, gesturing around the room which was filled with a bunch of twenty somethings. "You fit in fine. But I stick out like a sore thumb."

"No you don't!"

"I'm the only person here who's wearing a shirt with a collar! People will think you've brought your boring older brother out with you."

"No they won't." Samantha laughed. "And it doesn't matter anyway. Let's just have fun." She began to pull him in the direction of an arcade machine and he followed behind her with a reluctant smile.

They spent the next couple of hours playing on different machines and trying different cocktails. Wardell beat her on most of the games, but she didn't mind because they were having so much fun together.

Unfortunately, the night came to an embarrassing end when they attempted to go on the dodgems but only lasted about two minutes before the whole ride had to be completely shut down when Samantha's glasses flew off of her face after a car jolted into them on her side. The staff had to turn the lights on to their brightest setting whilst they helped Samantha look for her specs, and everyone stared and whispered to each other as if she was some kind of entertainment that had been hired for the evening.

As soon as the glasses were back on her face, she asked Wardell if they could go home.

"I can't believe that," she groaned whilst they walked back to his car. "Why do all the stupid things have to happen to me?"

Wardell couldn't stop laughing. "At least it's a fun story we can tell people about our first date."

Samantha rolled her eyes. "Awesome."

Wardell drove them back to his house and Samantha's eyes widened in surprise when she saw it for the first time as he was parking on his driveway.

"Oh my god. You live in a mansion."

Wardell chuckled. "It's not quite a mansion. It's only got three bedrooms."

"How many bathrooms has it got?"

"Just one, and then a downstairs toilet."

"Well, it's huge. By my standards anyway. I can't believe you've been coming to my flat all this time. You must hate it there."

"No, I love your flat. It's cosy."

Samantha wrinkled her nose at the backhanded compliment which was really just another way to describe it as small. "Yeah. Whatever." She followed him out of the car and then into the house, looking around in amazement once she saw the interior. "Wow. Being a private therapist must pay even better than I thought. You're really benefiting from all of my craziness."

He laughed again and came over to wrap his arms around her waist. "I'm benefitting from your craziness because it brought you into my life. Not because it helps me afford a nice house." He leaned down to kiss her softly, pulling away before it could go further. "I'll show you around."

He took her into his massive kitchen which had a fancy marble island in the centre of it, then he showed her the living room which had way too many seats in it for someone who lived alone, and finally he took her upstairs, briefly pointing out the two guest bedrooms before opening the door to his master one.

"This is your bedroom?" she asked in disbelief, staring at the king sized bed and built in double wardrobes. The room was the size of her living room, kitchen and bathroom put together. "This is nice. God, I bet that bed is comfy."

Wardell grinned and nodded his head towards the piece of furniture in question. "Try it out."

Samantha giggled and threw herself onto the luxurious looking comforter, feeling the mattress immediately begin to mould around her body. "I love this place," she told him

"Good." He suddenly crawled onto the bed and settled on top of her, leaning up on his elbows as he stared down at her with a look in his eye that she recognised well.

Samantha took his face between her hands and pulled his mouth down onto hers, tangling her tongue with his and moaning into his throat as she felt him begin to harden against her hip.

They slowly stripped each other of their clothes until they were both completely bare with every inch of their skin pressed together as they continued to kiss passionately.

Samantha had never experienced a more intimate moment and she suddenly felt a need to show Wardell just how much she cared for him and wanted him.

"Can I be on top this time?" she murmured against his mouth as she felt him begin to nudge at her entrance.

He pulled back with a sexy smile. "Yeah, if you want." He rolled them over so that he was on his back and she was looking down at him, and then connected their lips once more.

"Do you want me?" Samantha asked between kisses, using a line he usually used on her.

She got the reaction she'd wanted because Wardell groaned and his eyes grew even more heated. "Fuck yes, I want you."

Samantha fought back a smile and then sat up to get herself into position, gently grasping his erection and guiding it to her entrance, before slowly sliding down onto him until she could feel him as deep as it was possible to get.

"Fuck," Wardell muttered, pressing his head back into his pillow. "That feels good." He caught the smile on her face and gave her a questioning look. "What's wrong?"

"Nothing. I just like seeing this other side of you."

He laughed, making her insides tingle as his body shook against her. "I like *showing* you this other side of me."

Samantha pressed her hands against his muscular chest and started to lift herself off of him. Once only the tip of him was left inside of her, she stopped and hovered there teasingly before slamming back down and letting out a low moan in unison with Wardell as they felt just how amazing it was in that position.

As she continued to move over him, she mixed between going almost painfully slowly sometimes and then abruptly speeding up until she was fucking him like an animal, rutting her body against his as he held her hips tightly and thrust up into her.

"Oh, I think I'm getting close," she moaned as the familiar sensation started between her legs.

"Come on baby," he urged her, sliding his hand down from her hip to start rubbing circles around her clitoris. "Come for me."

It only took a couple of more strokes to take her over the edge, and then she was quivering on top of him, letting out breathy moans whilst struggling to still keep up the pace of her movements to help Wardell get to his own climax.

"Fuck, that's it," he groaned, squeezing her hips even more tightly and raising his upper half off of the bed so that they were almost face to face whilst he guided her over him in the rhythm he needed. "Shit, shit, shit."

He came loudly, burying his head into her neck and placing sloppy kisses there as she circled her arms around him and stroked his back comfortingly until both of their breathing had returned to normal.

Chapter Thirty Five

"Have you told your mum and dad about us?" Wardell asked a while later as they lay under the covers with Samantha's head resting on his chest.

She leaned up on her elbow to look at him properly. "No, not yet. I was going to probably tell them tomorrow when I go to their house for lunch. Why?"

He looked nervous all of a sudden. "I'm just a bit worried about what they might say."

"What do you mean?"

"Well, they might not like that you're going out with your therapist."

Samantha frowned. She hadn't considered her parents potentially having a problem with the relationship, but now that he'd mentioned it she worried he could be right. "Oh, well, I'm sure they'll be fine in the end. Even if they think it's weird at first, once I tell them how happy you make me they should be pleased."

Wardell smiled and ran his fingers up and down her bare back. "Yeah, I hope so."

Samantha was the first awake the next day and she smiled softly as she lay and watched him sleeping for a while.

He was such a beautiful man, and she still couldn't believe how lucky she was to have found him. Although they'd met in sad circumstances, she didn't regret it at all because it had brought them together.

As she snuggled closer to him, she felt his hardness digging into her stomach and slowly lifted the covers to examine the mighty length before suddenly coming up with an idea.

Trying her best to not wake him, she carefully rolled him onto his back and then straddled his body, moving down until her face was level with the straining erection.

So far, he had never asked her for a blow job, but she knew how much guys tended to like them and wanted to do something selfless to please him; especially after all the times he'd gone down on her and given her incredible orgasms.

Leaning down, she placed a soft kiss on his tip and then wrapped her lips around him and lowered her head further to allow him to slide down her throat.

Wardell made a strange noise, but a quick glance upwards confirmed that he was still asleep so Samantha tightened her mouth and began to suck and suck until finally his body jolted and he sat up, blinking sleepily down at her.

Once his brain processed what she was doing, his lips curved up into a smirk and he moved his hand to grip hold of her hair and help guide her as she moved her head up and down, gradually speeding up her rhythm as the noises he was making in the back of his throat spurred her on to finish him off.

"Fuck," he hissed. "That feels so fucking good Samantha."

His obvious pleasure made her grow warm and she started to feel a tingling between her legs which made her squirm against the mattress.

Wardell must have seen what she was doing because he soon growled, "Get up here," and she pulled away in confusion before finally understanding what he meant when he started to turn her around and position her on top of him so that his dick was still level with her face, but her wet flesh was within easy reach for him to tilt his head up and start to lick through her folds.

Samantha moaned at what he was doing to her, momentarily struggling to concentrate on what she was still doing to him before she then forced herself to focus and put even more effort into getting him off.

She knew when he was close because his hand suddenly pressed down on the back of her head, keeping her still as he started to gently thrust up into her mouth, hitting the back of her throat each time he did so.

"Ah! Fuck!" He shouted with his mouth still pressed against her, sending shivers through her core as his semen spurted into her mouth. She'd just managed to swallow it all down when her own orgasm overtook her, making her whole body tense as she panted loudly and curled her fingers into the duvet cover.

"Oh my god," she breathed as she collapsed onto her back beside Wardell once more. She turned her head to look at him shyly. "Was that okay for you?"

He gave her a lascivious grin, and she had her answer.

"You could come in with me if you want to?" Samantha suggested as she got dressed after their shower. He'd offered to drop her off at her mum and dad's house for lunch, but had said it was probably best for him to park around the corner so that they wouldn't see them together before Samantha had a chance to tell them the news.

Wardell raised his eyebrows. "Why? So that if your dad wants to hit me I'll be right there for him?"

Samantha laughed and rolled her eyes. "He's not gonna want to hit you. You're probably thinking too much into this. I bet they don't even care, and in a few hours I'll be making fun of you for being so overdramatic."

"Well," Wardell sighed. "I still don't think I should be there. But if you want, I'll pick you up when you're done and I can come in and see them then if it's gone well."

"Okay." Samantha smiled. "Sounds like a plan."

Chapter Thirty Six

"I'll see you later then," Wardell said as he pulled his car to a stop and leaned over the centre console to give Samantha a kiss goodbye. "Have a nice time."

She got out of the car and gave him one last wave before he drove off and she made her way to her mum and dad's house.

"Hi honey!" Her mum said cheerfully once she opened the door, pulling Samantha inside the house and engulfing her in a hug. "You look nice."

"Oh. Thanks." She couldn't remember the last time she'd received a compliment from her mother. She hadn't realised that just putting a bit of mascara on and wearing slightly nicer clothes would make such a big difference

Her dad came out from the kitchen, throwing a tea towel over his shoulder, and appraising his daughter in the same way her mum had. "You look nice."

Samantha almost rolled her eyes.

They sat down for lunch about ten minutes later, and an opportunity to tell her parents about her relationship with Wardell came sooner than she would have expected.

"So," her mum said as she cut up a piece of roast chicken. "Did you have your sessions with Wardell this week?"

"Er, yeah. On Monday and Friday as usual."

"It's so nice of him to keep seeing you for free. Isn't it Joe?"

Her dad agreed.

"You must have made a real impression on him," Elizabeth continued, wearing a proud mum face.

"Well," Samantha started nervously, putting her cutlery down so she could twist her hands together in her lap. "Um, me and Wardell have actually started dating."

The air in the room immediately grew tense as her parents stopped eating and stared at her in shock. Her mum's mouth had dropped open whilst her dad looked both angry and disgusted.

"Are you kidding me?" her mum asked eventually, looking at her husband in disbelief. "How long has this been going on?"

"Erm," Samantha quickly tried to think about whether it would be best to tell the whole truth or a white lie. She decided on the latter. "It's just been this week. Nothing ever happened between us when I was his proper patient."

Her dad scoffed, obviously not believing it. "Even if that's true, he was obviously still interested in you. He must have preyed on you."

"What?" Samantha was outraged on Wardell's behalf. "No he didn't!"

"How else do you explain it?" her mum chimed in. "He knows how ill you've been. He's supposed to have been trying to help you get better, not trying to seduce you!"

"And we've basically been paying him to do it!" her dad shouted, growing more angry. "How dare he take advantage of both us and *you* like that!"

"He's not taken advantage of anyone!"

"He's been taking our fucking money!"

Samantha fell speechless, not knowing how to handle being yelled at by her father.

"He's right," her mum said, taking over. "We should report him for this. It's an abuse of position."

"You can't!" Samantha protested, starting to panic at the suggestion. She'd never considered that they would get angry enough to want to do something as serious as that. "He's done nothing wrong. I pursued him, not the other way around."

Her dad's lip curled at that. "That doesn't matter. You've been mentally unwell. You were in a vulnerable position. Even if you did pursue him, he should have known better than to let anything happen."

"And let's not forget the age difference," her mum added. "How old is he?"

"He's thirty eight," Samantha said quietly.

"Eleven years older than you?" Her mum shook her head in disbelief. "Did you honestly expect us to be okay with this?"

"I thought you'd be happy for me. Wardell's helped me so much, and now we've developed feelings for each other. What's wrong with that?"

She hated the way her parents were looking at her as if she was a naive little girl.

"It's not right Samantha," her mum said with a sigh. "You're his patient. He should have stayed away from you. It's completely unprofessional."

"Will you just give him a chance?" Samantha pleaded, getting to her feet. "You loved him when you first met him. This shouldn't change your whole opinion of him. Look, he's picking me up in a bit. He said he was going to come in to say hello. Can you just please be nice to him? Let him prove to you what a nice guy he is, and show you that we're not doing anything wrong by being together. Especially when I'm not even his patient anymore."

Before either of her parents had a chance to answer, Samantha's phone chimed in her pocket, loud enough for them all to hear.

"Is that him?" her dad asked.

She pulled her phone out and glanced at the screen. "Yeah. he's asking what time he should come."

"Well tell him to come now. I want to hear what he has to say for himself."

Samantha reluctantly did as he said. Although she thought the whole thing was stupid, she also didn't want to wind her parents up anymore than they already were in case it drove them to follow through on the threat to report Wardell for misconduct.

Come now, she typed. *Just to warn you, they're not very happy. I'm sorry xx*

Wardell didn't respond, but she knew he'd read the message.

Less than ten minutes later, they heard his car pull up outside, and her parents positioned themselves in the centre of the room with their arms crossed and stern expressions on their faces whilst Samantha went to open the door.

Chapter Thirty Seven

"Hey," Samantha said with a shaky smile as she let Wardell in. She was surprised to find that he didn't look nervous. Instead, he walked past her and headed straight for her mum and dad, stopping only a couple of metres away from them and mirroring their stances.

"Hi Elizabeth. Joe." He nodded towards each of them in turn. "Go on then. What have you got to say?"

Her parents were clearly taken aback by his confidence and it took them both a moment to be able to form any words.

"I think you should be showing us a bit more respect than that," her dad said angrily. "How dare you come in here and act so cocky."

Wardell shrugged, looking unbothered. "I was expecting you to have a problem. But I'm not going to apologise or be ashamed of being with your daughter. For one thing, I'm almost thirty nine years old, and for another, I have nothing to be sorry about. I really like Samantha. Yes, she was my patient, and I never intended to grow feelings for her, but it happened and I'm glad that it did. If anything, I think we were meant to be in each other's lives. That's why it was *my* car she chose to step in front of."

Again, her mum and dad seemed lost for words. They had obviously expected Wardell to come in looking like an embarrassed little boy and begging them to not report him; but instead, he'd decided to face them like the mature man he really was.

"I'm not going to let you excuse this as fate," her mum said, raising her chin in a snobbish manner. "And anyway, none of that changes the fact that you've been taking our money for those sessions when you've just been using the time to seduce our daughter."

Wardell screwed his face up. "If this is just about the money, you can have every penny of it back. I don't care. But, whether you believe it or not, we've stayed completely professional in all of our appointments. I was serious when I said I wanted to help Samantha, and that's exactly what I've been doing. That's all you should care about."

Samantha watched as her parents shared a questioning look, as if they were silently asking each other's opinion on Wardell's speech.

Finally, her mum sighed. "We don't want our money back," she said reluctantly. "We're grateful for how you've helped Samantha. It's easy to see the difference in her compared to when she was in the hospital. But..." She trailed off.

"Are you *really* serious about her?" Samantha's dad cut in. "You're not just using her until you find another patient to go after?"

"No, of course not." From the tone Wardell used, it was impossible to think he was telling anything but the truth.

"Have you ever had a relationship with a patient before this?"

Samantha held her breath as she silently willed Wardell to lie instead of making the situation worse by telling them about Jersey.

"No. Samantha's my only patient that I've ever had feelings for," Wardell said, purposely wording his answer so that it wasn't a lie.

It seemed to be enough to satisfy her parents.

"Fine then," her dad said. "As long as there's nothing sordid going on, I suppose it's none of our business. Samantha's old enough now to decide who she wants to be with, and as long as you treat her right then we'll be happy."

Wardell nodded solemnly. "I will. You don't have to worry about that."

"So does this mean you're not going to report him?" Samantha asked. Wardell shot her a quick, wary glance; obviously shocked at the news that reporting him had ever been an option.

"No, we won't," her mum said reassuringly. She gave them both a pointed look. "But I think it's probably best if we all arrange to go out for a meal or something, so we can get to know Wardell as your boyfriend instead of just as your therapist."

Wardell gave her his most charming look, and Samantha could see that it had an effect on her mum, in the way she guessed it probably would on all women. "That's fine by me."

He turned away and winked secretively at Samantha, making her have to fight back a smirk.

He knew exactly what he was doing.

Chapter Thirty Eight

"My dad wants to meet you," Wardell announced the following Friday once he and Samantha had finished their therapy session at his house.

She raised her eyebrows in surprise. "You've told him about me?"

"Yeah," he smiled. "Why wouldn't I?"

"I don't know." She shrugged. "I just didn't know if you thought it was a big enough deal yet."

"Of course I do," he said with a frown, suddenly looking unsure. "I mean, *you* do, don't you?"

"Yeah." She leaned over to give him a quick kiss. "Sorry, I didn't mean to sound so negative. I'm pleased that you want me to meet your dad. I've never actually met a guy's family before."

"Really?"

"Yeah. I've never been out with someone long enough."

Wardell wrapped his arm around her and pulled her into his side. "Those guys were stupid. They didn't deserve you."

Samantha flushed at the compliment. "So, have you introduced your dad to a lot of girls over the years?"

He shook his head. "No. Just the one. Celeste, my ex fiance."

"No one else?"

"Nope. I was with Celeste for five years and since her, like I said, I've not met anyone I cared about too much."

Samantha nudged him teasingly with her shoulder. "But you care about me?"

"I *more* than care about you." His expression suddenly turned serious. "I think I'm very quickly falling in love with you."

A smile spread across her face, so wide that it made her cheeks hurt. "I think I am too."

They began to kiss, slowly at first and then gradually speeding up until they were moaning into each other's mouths and pulling at clothes in an obvious indication that they both wanted to take things to the next level.

Keeping their lips attached, they stood up from the couch and moved towards the stairs, stumbling up them before they then tripped and landed in a heap right at the top.

"Sorry," Wardell laughed as he fell on her. He got back to his feet and reached out a hand to help her up.

"It's okay." Samantha looped her arms around his neck and kissed him again, tugging up the bottom of his t-shirt until he got the hint and removed it.

"You too," he told her with a dark look in his eyes. He watched intently as she stripped out of her clothes. "And your underwear." She did as he commanded.

Wardell quickly took his own jeans and boxers off and kicked them away so that they were both left standing completely nude at the top of the stairs.

"Bend over the bannister," he ordered her in a lust filled voice.

Samantha was shocked by the sudden transition away from the usual sex they had, but she was more than a little intrigued by the idea of trying out the new position.

Without needing any further encouragement, she turned around and bent over as he'd said, holding on to the wood of the bannister to keep her balance.

"Fuck, you look good like that," Wardell murmured behind her. She felt him step closer and press his erection against her, rubbing it slowly between her legs in a teasing movement.

"Ugh, put it in," Samantha moaned.

She heard him laugh before he then grasped tightly onto her hips and thrust into her body in one quick, hard stroke."

"Oh fuck," he groaned, repositioning her slightly and then beginning to slam in and out of her in an almost frantic rhythm.

Samantha loved it. Nothing had ever felt so good to her before and she couldn't help but make repetitive, animalistic sounds as she pushed back against Wardell whilst he fucked her uncontrollably.

"Oh god, I'm already close," she panted, squeezing her eyes shut as she did her best to try and hold her orgasm back in order to make the experience last longer.

"Me too," he told her, speaking in a strange voice as if he too was restraining himself. "I want you to come with me, okay?"

She nodded desperately. "I can't hold it much longer."

"It's okay baby. Let go. Come for me. Now."

They both called out at the exact same time, and then trembled against each other whilst their climaxes rocketed through them.

Once Samantha had stopped shaking, and there was nothing left for Wardell to release, they sank to the ground, still joined, and curled their sweaty bodies together.

Chapter Thirty Nine

Samantha could barely sit still on the drive over to Wardell's dad's house.

She hadn't realised she would be so nervous at the prospect of meeting a boyfriend's parent, but after her own parent's bad reaction to their relationship, she was suddenly worried that they would get an equally bad reception from Clive. Wardell had said his father was excited to meet her, but she was still concerned that once he actually spoke to her he might change his mind and that, in turn, there was a possibility that her boyfriend could change his too.

"We're here," Wardell announced as he pulled into the driveway of a modest, semi-detached house. He gave her an amused look. "Don't be nervous. It'll be fine. I promise. My dad's a nice guy. And he already knows about you being my patient and everything, so there's no surprises for him to find out about."

Samantha blew out a long breath. "Okay, let's go then."

When Clive opened his front door for them a moment later, she could tell immediately that he was a kind man. Something about the warm smile on his face and the creases by his eyes as he looked at his son made her see the handsome young man that he must have once been, and the pride he felt as a father.

"Wardell," he said brightly, wrapping his arms around his son and rubbing his back affectionately. "Good to see you."

Samantha smiled at the display. It was always nice to see such a close family, and the fact that she knew Wardell saw his dad once a week and yet they still made a big deal out of his visits just made the whole thing even better.

"Dad, this is Samantha," Wardell said, stepping away and wrapping his arm supportively around her waist. "Samantha, this is my dad. Clive."

"Hi, nice to meet you," she said quietly, with an awkward smile.

"You too." He reached out to shake her hand but then surprised her by pulling her into a firm hug as well. "Wardell's told me so much about you."

"He's told me a lot about you too."

The three of them walked inside of his house and she was given a quick tour before they finally settled on the couches in the living room.

"So, I hope you don't mind, but I'm not very good at cooking, so I was thinking we could just order a takeaway or something. What do you think?"

He directed the question towards Samantha and she nodded timidly. "Yeah, that's fine with me."

"Good."

Whilst Clive went off to order their food, a picture on top of the fireplace suddenly caught Samantha's eye and she stood up to go and inspect it.

"Is this you?" she asked Wardell, grinning at the image of a young toddler with a cheeky face and mismatched clothing.

He came to look over her shoulder. "Yep. That's me. Great fashion sense in the eighties."

"You're cute," Samantha insisted, unable to stop herself from wondering if *their* children would look just as adorable if their relationship went well and they got to that stage.

"Thanks." He took the frame off her and placed it back in its original position. "There's some more pictures on the wall going up the stairs, if you want to see?"

Samantha nodded eagerly. "Show me."

"Well that went well," Samantha said a couple of hours later as they drove away from Clive's house.

"I told you it would." Wardell reached across the car and took her hand in his, squeezing it gently. "My dad's not a judgemental person."

"He's a really nice man," Samantha said with a fond smile. "It's kind of sad that he's all alone. Has he had any serious relationships since your mum left?"

Wardell shrugged. "Not really. I think he's dated a few women over the years, but he was never really interested in wanting to marry again or anything."

"That's a shame."

He gave her a teasing look. "Are you gonna try and matchmake? Find my dad a woman?"

"No." Samantha laughed. "I'm just saying that it doesn't feel fair that he's been on his own all these years."

"He doesn't mind. I think he actually kind of liked being a single dad."

"Well, either way, you're lucky to have him."

Wardell smiled. "I know I am." He squeezed her hand once more. "And I'm lucky to have *you* as well."

Samantha blushed. "I'm glad we can finally relax and just enjoy being together now."

"Yeah, I know. Me too. There's nothing more to worry about."

But they were going to discover that they'd spoken too soon.

There was *much* more to worry about.

In fact, the worst was yet to come....

Chapter Fourty

For the next couple of weeks, everything was perfect.

Samantha and Wardell spent practically every free minute of their time together, and Samantha's tablets continued to work on improving her mood until she was almost back to the girl she remembered being many years before.

Wardell was still strict in making sure they kept to their regular Monday and Friday appointments together, and he was there to help her whenever she felt low or was stuck in a loop of checking that she found difficult to break, so overall her life was vastly better.

The only bleak point was the jealousy she felt towards Jersey.

She knew that Wardell still had regular sessions with her, and when she'd asked him a bit about them she'd found out that Jersey constantly tried to flirt with him and hinted that she wanted a repeat of their one night stand, so it bothered

Samantha that he had to spend so much time alone with the girl.

Although she trusted that he would never cheat on her, she still didn't like it; especially when Wardell had told her how temperamental Jersey was.

"I can't risk her reporting me," he told her one day when she asked again about the possibility of him making some excuse and getting rid of her as his patient.

"Well, is there nothing you could do to try and convince her to get rid of *you* as her therapist?"

"Like what?"

Samantha thought for a moment but then sighed. "I don't know. I just don't like the idea of her pestering you all the time. I mean, you reject her constantly so why's she not given up by now?"

"I have no idea," Wardell said, seeming perplexed. "Sometimes I think she just likes the chase. I think she likes to see it as a kind of game that we're playing together. I don't know, maybe she's even convinced herself that I'm just playing hard to get."

The girl sounded delusional, but Samantha didn't say so out loud. She knew she'd be a hypocrite to criticise someone else about their mental health.

"Well, just be careful," she told him. "Don't let her blackmail you or anything."

Wardell pulled her close and pressed a kiss against her lips. "I won't."

Their troubles started one day when they decided to go shopping in the city centre. They'd both just been paid and Samantha wanted to get herself some new, sexy underwear to take advantage of the fact that she now had someone to see it on a regular basis. She wanted to impress Wardell with something fancy, instead of just wearing her old plain bras and unmatching knickers, so she dragged him out with her and had him help her to choose some.

It was as they were in a lingerie shop and Wardell was messing around by holding up different skimpy garments in front of her that they suddenly heard a bewildered voice say, "Doctor Briggs?"

Samantha and Wardell snapped their heads around and saw Jersey standing a few feet away, watching them with a suspicious look in her eyes.

"Oh, hi Jersey." Wardell quickly hung up the corset he was holding and shoved his hands into his pockets before turning to his patient and giving her a forced smile. "Doing a bit of shopping?"

"Er, yeah." She flicked her gaze between the pair of them. "What are *you* doing? Who's she?"

Samantha was finding it hard to not glare at the other girl, but she did her best to keep her expression neutral as Jersey's eyes began to examine her closely.

"Err, this is my girlfriend," Wardell said. "Samantha."

"Girlfriend?" Jersey looked horrified, and she immediately narrowed her eyes and curled her lip as she shot Samantha a poisonous look. "Since when did you have a girlfriend? You've never told me about this."

Wardell frowned. "Well, why would I?"

Jersey looked offended by the question. She obviously thought she had a right to know what was going on in Wardell's life.

A smirk curved her mouth as her eyes lit up with an idea and she fixed her gaze on Samantha once more. "We fucked, you know."

Samantha fought the urge to slap her and she was careful to keep her mouth closed so that she wouldn't say something that she'd later regret.

"Jersey," Wardell said in a warning tone. "I don't think that's really relevant, is it? It was years ago."

She scowled, apparently not liking him diminishing what they'd shared. "Whatever. I bet you would have fucked me again if I wasn't your patient." The words triggered a memory in her brain and Samantha saw the exact moment that she finally recognised just who exactly she was. "Wait a minute, *you're* his patient too, aren't you? I saw you that time in the waiting room." She widened her eyes at Wardell, giving him a hurt look. "How could you?"

"Jersey." He held his hands up defensively as he started to speak in a placating tone. "I told you there was nothing between us. It wasn't only your status as my patient that made me not want to be with you."

"Fuck you," she spat, before then turning her hateful stare on Samantha. "And fuck you too, you stupid whore."

"Don't speak to her like that," Wardell warned, taking a step sideways to stand in front of Samantha in a protective stance. "This is none of your business Jersey."

She scowled. "Maybe not. But I think your bosses would be interested to know this. And to know that you fucked me as well."

Wardell froze. "Are you threatening me?"

"Yep." She was completely unashamed. "I'm not going to let you treat me like this and get away with it."

It was almost disturbing for Samantha to hear how delusional Jersey was. She wanted to step in and say something, but knew it was probably best to leave the talking to Wardell who had experience of dealing with difficult people.

"Calm down Jersey," he told her. "I've not done anything to you. There was never anything going on between us."

"But you fucked me!" Her voice had started to get louder and Samantha noticed a few nosy people looking towards them. "How can you say nothing was going on between us? And anyway, no matter what you think, it doesn't change that it's against the rules for you to go around sleeping with your patients. I can make you lose your job. You'll never be allowed alone with a patient again."

"Don't do that Jersey. Samantha's not even my patient anymore, and do you really want to lose me as your therapist? Would you really ruin my life like that after everything I've helped you through?"

Jersey finally started to look unsure, and Samantha almost sagged in relief as she realised that Wardell was managing to get through to her.

He seemed to have a real knack for talking people down from a ledge.

Jersey sighed grudgingly. "No, Wardell, of course I don't want to ruin your career. You know I love you."

Samantha's nostrils flared at hearing those words come out of the other girl's mouth.

"But I can't stand the thought of you being with anyone but me," Jersey continued in a whiny voice. "I mean, can't you give *us* a chance."

Wardell seemed to be grinding his teeth. "No, Jersey. That's not going to happen."

There was a finality in Wardell's tone that hadn't been there before, and Jersey obviously noticed it because her face began to look red and it seemed that she might actually explode.

However, when she finally spoke, her voice was deathly quiet. "Fine," was all she said before abruptly turning and flouncing away.

Samantha and Wardell both watched her disappear and then turned back to one another.

"What do you think she's gonna do?" Samantha asked. "Do you think she'll report you?"

Wardell shook his head, looking bewildered. "I honestly have no idea. We're just going to have to wait and see."

Chapter Fourty One

Samantha opened her eyes the next day to find Wardell already awake and watching her with a gentle smile on his face.

"Good morning," he murmured.

"Morning."

"You look so peaceful when you're asleep."

"Really? I always imagined I'd look like this." She pulled a stupid face, causing them both to burst out laughing.

"No," Wardell finally said. "You look a lot more beautiful than that."

It didn't take them long to start kissing, and before Samantha knew it, Wardell had rolled on top of her and was sliding into her body, making her gasp against his mouth in the way she always did.

They'd had *a* lot of sex so far, and yet she was still always surprised by just how *good* it felt.

"Do you want it slow?" he asked her, gazing into her eyes as he began to move in and out.

She nodded her head and then lifted her legs to wrap around his waist, gently rotating her hips against him as she felt him slide even deeper.

They were both getting better at trying to hold their orgasms back in order to prolong sex, so it took almost half an hour before Samantha started to feel the familiar stirring at the pit of her stomach.

"Ah," she panted, giving him a hungry kiss as she bucked slowly upwards.

"Is it coming?" he asked, watching her intently.

"Oh." She moaned. "Yeah. I'm close."

"Me too."

They fell over the edge together and Wardell slipped his tongue into her mouth to kiss her slowly as their bodies shook and they shared a moment of pure bliss.

When he leaned back a few moments later, he gazed into her eyes in a way he never had before. "I love you Samantha," he told her softly.

The words hung in the air between them as excitement fizzed in Samantha's stomach. She'd been eagerly awaiting the day when he'd admit that 'falling in love' had turned into *actual* love, and she relished the chance to finally be able to tell him her own feelings.

"I love you too, Wardell."

Once they'd finally forced themselves out of bed, they had a shower together which ended with Wardell on his knees and Samantha trying her best to keep from sliding down the wall as he buried his face between her legs.

As they got dressed together afterwards, stopping to share a kiss every now and then, Wardell's phone suddenly rang. He reached to pick it up and Samantha watched as his face paled as he looked at whatever was on the screen.

"What's wrong?" she asked him.

"It's my boss," Wardell said in a quiet voice. They shared a panicked look. There was only one reason they could think of as to why his boss would be calling him on a Sunday.

Samantha stood there anxiously as he slid his finger across the screen to answer and lifted the phone to his ear with an unsteady hand. "Hello?"

He listened for a few moments with wide eyes and then his whole body suddenly stiffened. "What? That's not true." He shot Samantha a strange look and then abruptly turned and left the room, obviously wanting to finish the conversation in private.

She listened nervously as he paced up and down the hallway, sometimes murmuring into the phone and then at other times raising his voice.

What the hell was happening?

Was he already being sacked, without any kind of investigation beforehand?

It was almost ten minutes before the phone call finally ended and Wardell walked back into the room, looking like he was about to throw up.

"What's happening?" Samantha asked, twisting her hands together anxiously. "Has Jersey reported you? What did your boss say?"

Wardell swallowed audibly. "He suspended me."

Her stomach sank. "How long for? Are they investigating you for misconduct?"

"Yeah," he said quietly. "But it's not just them. The police are investigating me as well. Apparently they're going to be contacting me to come in for a voluntary interview."

"*The police? Why?*"

He met her eyes and she couldn't help but notice the fear in his expression.

"Jersey's accused me of rape."

Chapter Fourty Two

"What?" Samantha was horrified. "Why would she do that? I mean, reporting you to your bosses is one thing, but *rape*?"

"I know." He shook his head, seeming as if he was still trying to process what he'd been told. "She's....I never expected she'd do something like this." He ran his hands through his hair. "I mean, trying to destroy my career is one thing, but trying to get me *arrested*?"

"Surely she can't do this? There's no basis for the allegation! Surely the police will just ignore it?"

Wardell gave her a sad look. "They'll still have to look into it before they decide that. And by that time, my reputation and my job might have already been ruined."

"Well, what has she said exactly?"

He sighed, closing his eyes briefly as though trying to compose himself. "She's said I forced myself on her multiple times at the end of our sessions. And she's told them about my relationship with you to give the story a bit more credibility."

"Credibility?"

"Yeah. It's a good tactic really. Telling a truth as part of the lie to make the lie seem more believable. Once they find out that I really am in a relationship with another patient, they'll probably think I'm capable of doing what she's accused me of."

"But there's a big difference between them," Samantha said, still not wanting to believe that it was really happening. "I mean, dating one patient doesn't automatically mean you'd rape another."

"I know, but it probably makes me look suspicious enough to warrant a more in depth investigation that's likely to take longer." He rubbed his hands over his face. "It could take months before I'm in the clear."

Samantha looked around helplessly, wishing she knew what to say or do to try and make things better. "Well, have you not got anything you can show the police to prove that Jersey has been harassing you? Text messages or something?"

"No, unfortunately. She's only ever mithered me in person, during our sessions."

"Shit."

"Yep."

"So, what happens now then?"

He chewed on his lip, thinking. "I'm gonna call the police," he said quietly. "Maybe it will make me look better if I contact them first instead of them having to seek me out."

Samantha watched sadly as he picked his phone back up from the bed and walked dejectedly from the room.

Chapter Fourty Three

Wardell went to the police station for a voluntary interview the next day.

Samantha hated that she couldn't go there with him and that she had to go to work instead. Acting like she cared about doing stupid admin work was hard on a normal day, but it was worse when her boyfriend could possibly be being charged with a crime he didn't commit at the same time that she was there.

She checked her phone constantly throughout the afternoon, waiting for the moment when he got out of the interview and could finally call her to tell her what had happened; but she was confused when it got to her finishing time and he still hadn't been in contact. His appointment had been scheduled for almost five hours before, so she didn't understand how he could still be there.

Deciding to try calling him herself, she pulled her phone out as she waited for her bus to arrive. As she listened to it ringing over and over in her ear, she expected him to not answer, so was surprised when his voice suddenly came over the line just before it cut off and went to voicemail.

"Hey Samantha." He sounded unbelievably tired.

"Hey, where are you?"

"At home."

She frowned. "When did your interview finish?"

"About three 'o' clock."

"Oh. Why didn't you call me?"

He sighed. "Sorry. I didn't want to disturb you at work. I thought it would be best to talk once you were finished."

Something in his tone made her stomach cramp. "Wardell, what's going on? What happened?"

"Well, they arrested me and read me my rights as soon as I got there," he told her, sounding as if he was reciting the story on autopilot. "Then they got me a Duty Solicitor and I was interviewed for over an hour, and then they released me under investigation."

"Oh my god." Samantha let her bus drive past her and sank down onto a bench. "Are you okay? How do you feel?"

He let out a sardonic laugh. "I don't even know. I mean, I'm suspended from work, I've been arrested, I've got bail conditions to not contact Jersey. I feel like a criminal."

"But you're not!" Samantha reminded him. "You've done nothing wrong, so they can't possibly charge you. It'll all be fine in the end."

"I hope so."

She hated the despair she heard in his voice. "Do you want me to come to your house? I'll order you a takeaway and do my best to cheer you up."

"No thanks."

"Oh." Her cheeks flushed at the rejection, although she understood why he wanted to be alone. "Okay. But call me if you want to talk or anything."

Wardell cleared his throat. "Actually Samantha, I think it's probably best if we stay away from each other for a while."

Her body went cold. "What do you mean? Why?"

"I think it would just be better that way. I don't really want you involved in all of this."

She fought back tears. "But I'm already involved. They know about me and you. Staying away from each other isn't going to change anything."

"It might," he said glumly. "I could tell Jersey we've split up. Maybe she'd withdraw her statement then."

"Do you really think that will work?"

"I don't know." She got the feeling he likely had his eyes squeezed shut or was running his fingers madly through his hair. "But I think it's worth a try. It might help with my job as well. And I just think it would be easier on both of us if you weren't in the middle of everything. I can't really....be your boyfriend when I've got all of this going on."

Samantha stayed silent, knowing that if she opened her mouth she would probably start sobbing.

"I'm not saying I want to break up," Wardell reassured her once he realised she wasn't going to say anything. "I just think we should pause the relationship until I've got all of this sorted and Jersey has backed off. I mean, who knows, if she's willing to do something like this to me, she might try and do something to you as well. I don't want that to happen, okay? I want to protect you, and this is the only thing I can think of."

Tears had started to slowly roll down her cheeks and although she hated what he was suggesting, she had to admit that she understood why he thought it would be a good idea. She hadn't considered the possibility of Jersey targeting her until then, but now that he'd mentioned it, she thought it was a real possibility; especially if the other girl thought she and Wardell were still together.

"Okay, fine," she said, trying her best to not sound like she was crying. "I'll stay away. But *please* keep me updated with what's going on, alright? And tell me the minute the police drop their investigation."

"I will, believe me." She heard the smile in his voice, and it reassured her that he wasn't just finding an excuse to break up with her. He was doing it because he *loved* her.

That knowledge would be enough to keep her going until she could finally see him again.

Chapter Fourty Four

Samantha didn't hear from Wardell for eleven days.

At first, she'd just waited by the phone, hoping that it would suddenly start ringing or that she'd receive a text, but once a week had passed with no contact, she started trying to call and text him.

He never replied.

She hated not knowing what was going on or even where he was. He was still her boyfriend, after all, and she wanted to be there for him in his time of need. So why was he shutting her out?

Why hadn't he so much as text her to ask how she was?

When she got a knock on her door early in the morning on the twelfth day, she rushed to answer it, knowing it could only be him.

He grinned widely when he saw her, in the affectionate way that she'd missed, and then without a word of explanation, he stepped into the flat, shut her door behind him and crushed his lips down onto hers.

Samantha couldn't help but moan into his mouth as he started to walk her backwards, leading them both to her bedroom. She let out a slight noise of surprise when they suddenly fell onto her bed, and then Wardell covered her mouth with his again and prevented her from making any further noise.

It didn't take long for their clothes to come off and for him to thrust inside of her, groaning loudly as he began to fuck her like some kind of animal who'd been starved of sex for months instead of just eleven days.

"Oh god Samantha," he panted, staring intensely down into her eyes as she writhed beneath him. "I love you so fucking much. This feels so fucking good."

She could only moan in response as she felt the beginnings of an orgasm brewing between her thighs.

Wardell suddenly lifted her legs in the air and pushed them forwards so that her knees were by her ears. The new position felt amazing and she was soon screaming out as she climaxed.

Due to how dazed she was from the pleasure, she was only half aware of what was going on when Wardell abruptly pulled out of her and began stroking his dick to finish himself off. As the evidence of his release splashed onto her face whilst he knelt over her groaning loudly, she only then started to feel surprised and slightly unnerved about why he'd decided to mix things up; especially without asking her about it first.

They lay in each other's arms after he'd fetched a wipe to clean her up, and she struggled to decide which of her many questions to ask first.

Thinking it would be best to go with the easiest one, she asked, "Why didn't you come inside me? Why'd you do it on my face like that?"

Instead of looking embarrassed or contrite, he smirked. "I don't know. I just kind of wanted to mark you as mine. I suppose it's a sort of primal thing." He frowned, suddenly looking worried. "You were alright with it, weren't you? I mean, I've missed you so much, and having that time apart just made me realise how much I'd hate to lose you properly, so that's why I did it. To claim you. I'm sorry. Is that stupid?"

His speech made Samantha smile. Although she knew some girls would probably find what he'd done pathetic and would say that he shouldn't act like he owned her, she couldn't help but be pleased by his possessiveness.

"No. That's not stupid," she said, planting a kiss on his cheek. "So, will you explain to me why you're here now? Has something happened? Or did you just miss me?"

He smiled broadly, in a way which didn't particularly suit the topic of conversation. "Well, actually, I'm here because Jersey retracted her statement."

Samantha gasped. "Really? Oh my god!" She threw herself towards him, hugging him tightly as they laughed happily together. "When did that happen?"

"Yesterday."

"This is amazing!" She almost couldn't believe that he was telling the truth. That their problems had been fixed so easily. "Do you know why she did it? Or did the police find out she was lying? Did they make her withdraw the allegation?"

There was the briefest pause before Wardell shrugged. "I'm not sure. They didn't say, and I didn't bother asking because I only cared about my name being cleared."

Samantha smiled. "It doesn't matter anyway. As long as you're free and we can be together properly again." They shared another hug. "I've missed you so much."

He kissed her temple. "I've missed you too baby."

Chapter Fourty Five

Unfortunately, Wardell was told that his suspension from work wouldn't be ending just because the police weren't taking any further action with his case. His boss said that they were still investigating him about his relationship with Samantha, and still needed to decide if his misconduct warranted him losing his job altogether.

Wardell was trying his best to seem like he wasn't worried too much about it, but Samantha could see that he was scared.

"Nothing's as bad as getting arrested," he told her, convincing himself as much as her. "As long as that part's over, I can deal with anything else."

Of course, he continued to give Samantha her hour long sessions on a Monday and Friday, and he assured her that he would always be there to help her in the future regardless of what happened with his job.

It was as they were lying in his bed in a post-coital state after her appointment the following Friday that his doorbell started to ring with one continuous chime, as if someone was pressing down on the button without letting go.

Wardell groaned. "Who the fuck is that?" He tightened his arms around Samantha. "I don't want to move. I'm comfy."

She laughed. "Do you want me to get it?"

"No, it's okay. I'll go." He didn't move.

"Wardell?"

"Mmm."

The doorbell was still ringing and it was starting to get really annoying so Samantha climbed out of the bed and quickly pulled her jeans on. She looked around for her t-shirt but couldn't find it so just slipped on Wardell's shirt because it was the closest thing to her.

With a sigh, she made her way out of the room and down the stairs. "I'm coming. Shut up," she grumbled as whoever it was became even more persistent and started banging on the door with their fist.

Samantha pulled it open, getting ready to shout at the unwanted visitor, but quickly froze in shock when she saw who was standing there.

"What the fuck are *you* doing here?" Jersey snarled.

Chapter Fourty Six

"What are *you* doing here?" Samantha asked in return. "How do you even know where Wardell lives?"

Jersey ignored her question and just asked, "Where is he?" She barged her way into the house. "Wardell! Wardell!"

They heard his heavy footsteps hurrying down the stairs a few moments later, and he appeared in front of them wearing only his jeans. He must not have had time to find another shirt after Samantha put his on.

"Jersey!" His eyes were wide as he stared at the girl who had recently accused him of rape. "What are you doing here?"

"I wanted to see you," she said in a suddenly much quieter voice. "I missed you." She seemed to remember Samantha's presence. "Why's *she* here?"

"Um." Wardell looked nervously between both girls and Samantha saw his throat move with a gulp.

"You're not back together with her, are you?" Jersey asked, clenching her fists as she stared at him with accusing eyes. "You told me it was over between you."

Samantha began to worry about Jersey's overreaction to finding her in Wardell's house. She wondered if the only reason the other girl had retracted her statement was because she thought she no longer had any competition, and that therefore if she found out they were 'back together' she might want to press forward with her original accusations.

They needed to tread carefully, but Samantha had no idea how to do that so she cast a helpless look towards Wardell, indicating for him to take charge of the situation.

"Jersey." He sighed. "I think we should talk about this privately. Come in the kitchen and I'll explain everything, okay?"

"Are you *dumping* me?" Jersey screeched. "Seriously? After everything?"

Samantha reached the end of her tether. "He's not dumping you! You were never together in the first place! And you've ruined any chance of still being his patient by making up those lies about him!"

Jersey snapped her head round to glare at her. "We were never together?" She let out a humourless laugh. "So why was I in his bed this time last week? Why was he fucking me senseless?"

Chapter Fourty Seven

Samantha's blood ran cold but the shred of sanity she still had stopped her from lunging at Jersey and trying to rip her hair out.

She cast a quick look at Wardell, her supposed boyfriend, and knew immediately from the terrified expression on his face that Jersey had been telling the truth.

She wanted to shout. She wanted to scream. But instead she stayed scarily calm as she settled her gaze back on the girl who had just destroyed her relationship, and kept her tone neutral as she said, "Get out."

Jersey scoffed. "No. I'm not going anywhere. It's me Wardell wants to be with now. Not you."

"No, I don't!" Wardell shouted exasperatedly. "Jersey, go home. Last week meant nothing, okay? You know why I did it. I told you I didn't want to see you ever again afterwards, so go home!"

"You fucking bastard!" Jersey was seething. "Why did you act all nice afterwards, if it meant nothing? Why were you cuddling and kissing me? Were you just tricking me? Making sure I went to the police and got them to drop the case before you told me to leave you alone?"

Wardell's face hardened. "Yes, that's exactly what I was doing. Why else do you think my reply to you telling me you'd been to the police station was to tell you to stay out of my life?"

Jersey held her forehead as if it was hurting her to put the pieces together and see the full story. Samantha watched her with concern; not for the girl herself, but she was worried that Jersey might lash out at either her or Wardell.

"I'm gonna go back to the police," she threatened once she'd got her composure back. "I'll tell them you blackmailed me into withdrawing the accusation. I'll get them to charge you properly."

Wardell only laughed and shook his head, seeming unworried. "They won't believe you, even if you did do that," he said. "You've proven you're unreliable now." He stepped closer towards her so that he was towering over her form. "And, don't forget, I could always tell them that *you* blackmailed *me* as well."

Jersey's face was bright red with anger by that point, and she spluttered for a moment, trying to think of a decent comeback, but then finally gave up.

"You're not getting away with this Wardell," she warned before turning her back to him and marching out of the house, slamming the door behind her.

Once Samantha and Wardell were left alone, he turned to her with imploring eyes.

"Baby...I'm sorry." He reached his arms out for her but she quickly stepped back.

"Don't touch me," she growled. "What did you *do*, Wardell?"

He sighed. "Jersey called me one day last week. She said she was willing to tell the police to drop the case, but she said she wanted me to fuck her again first."

Tears came to her eyes. "So you just agreed?"

He shook his head. "No, I refused at first." His shoulders slumped. "But then I got so worried about what was going to happen, and I started to convince myself that I would end up being one of those people that go to prison for something they didn't do so...I gave in. I told her I'd do it."

The first tear dripped down her cheek. "How could you do that to me?"

"I'm sorry! I thought it was the only way to get her to leave us alone, but I should have realised she'd start getting carried away with herself afterwards." He rubbed his hands over his face in frustration. "I just wanted everything to be okay again."

"You thought *cheating* on me would make everything okay?" She wiped some of the wetness from her cheeks, but more soon replaced it. "Were you even going to tell me?"

Wardell shook his head sadly. "I didn't want you to know." He took a tentative step towards her again. "Samantha, please forgive me. I promise you it didn't mean anything. I hated every minute of it."

"That doesn't matter! It doesn't change the fact you slept with her, in this house of all places. In the bed that we've just had sex in. It doesn't change that you've been *inside* of her." A thought suddenly came to her mind and she looked at him with wide eyes. "Wait a minute, you slept with her, but you've not been using protection with me? You could have given me something you idiot!"

"No, no, it's fine," he rushed to reassure her. "I used a condom with Jersey, and anyway, she's not slept with anyone else but me since she first became my patient. She's told me that loads of times."

She gave him a sceptical look. "Really? Are you sure about that? Are you sure the reason you pulled out last week wasn't because of her?"

Wardell screwed up his face. "No! I told you what that was about! But, yes, I suppose in a way it was because of her. I felt guilty about what I'd done and I was worried about losing you, so I did it to leave my mark on you, like I said. It wasn't for any other reason."

Samantha let out a sigh of relief, pleased that she at least had one less thing to worry about.

"What are you thinking?" Wardell asked when she hadn't spoken for a couple of minutes whilst she tried to straighten everything in her mind.

She reluctantly met his eyes, immediately feeling a sensation like a punch to the chest as she examined the man she loved.

"I don't know what to think," she admitted. "I thought everything was alright now, other than your job..."

"It is alright," Wardell cut in. "We don't have to let Jersey ruin what we have if we don't want her to. We can move on from it. Pretend it never happened."

"But it *did* happen, Wardell." She scowled. "And you're the one that's ruined everything, not me."

"I'm sorry!" He wrapped his arms around her even though she tried to resist. "Please. I love you, and you love me. I don't feel anything for Jersey. I *hate* her. I did what I did for *us*."

She raised her eyebrows. "Oh, well thanks for that," she said sarcastically before shoving out of his embrace and walking upstairs to collect the rest of her things from his room.

"What are you doing?" he asked, following her.

"I'm leaving. I don't want you anywhere near me."

"No Samantha!" He stood in the bedroom doorway, stopping her from going back downstairs. "Let's talk more about this. You know I didn't betray you. Not really. I just *had* to do it. I couldn't bear to be accused of something like that. I was desperate!"

"I don't care!" She screamed in his face. "You cheated on me. That's all that matters."

His eyes became watery. "No, it's about more than that. What would you have done in my position? Would you have just let someone ruin your life? Or would you have been willing to do whatever it took to make the problem go away?"

Samantha didn't have an answer for him.

"Wardell," she sighed. "I need to think, okay? Will you please just let me leave?"

He hesitated for a moment but then stepped aside, allowing Samantha to bolt past him and make her escape.

Chapter Fourty Eight

Samantha ignored every attempt Wardell made to contact her over the next week. She deleted his texts and voicemails without listening to them, and didn't turn up for her scheduled sessions at his house on Monday and Friday.

Even when he came round to her flat and either rang her buzzer or knocked on her door for almost an hour, she ignored him and pretended she wasn't home, waiting for him to get the point and leave, which he always inevitably did.

She was still angry about his betrayal and had no desire to speak to him until she'd come to a final decision about whether she really wanted to end their relationship or not.

On Sunday afternoon, she wasn't surprised when the knocking started again, and she put her book down on the table with a sigh, knowing she wouldn't be able to read it with the constant pounding going on in the background.

After a couple of minutes, however, she frowned when her phone beeped with an incoming message from Wardell.

I miss you baby. Please call me. We need to talk about this xx

Why was he texting her like that when he was standing right outside her door?

It was only then that she suddenly realised that the knocking wasn't the same as usual. It had a different rhythm to it, and somehow didn't sound like it was Wardell's fist that was making the noise.

Curious, she got up from the couch and went to look through the peephole.

Jersey was outside.

"What the hell?" she muttered to herself as she pulled the door open. "How did you find me?"

"I followed you after you left Wardell's house last weekend," Jersey told her with a smirk, completely unashamed about admitting something like that.

"Well, what do you want?"

Jersey just stared at her in a way that was very unsettling; like some kind of demon in a horror movie, trying to scare its victim before making its ultimate move.

"Hello? Are you gonna say anything?" Samantha crossed her arms, getting annoyed. "Look, if you're just going to try and creep me out, I'm closing the door."

"Don't do that," Jersey suddenly said. "I want to talk to you."

"About what?"

She cocked her head. "You're ugly. I don't know why Wardell likes you."

"Okay..."

"He's not going to like you for long, though. I'm going to make sure of it."

Samantha raised her eyebrows. "So, you're threatening *me* now?"

Jersey didn't answer and instead just lifted the water bottle she'd had dangling by her side and held it out like an offering. "Do you want a drink?"

"No." Samantha frowned. Was the girl on *drugs* or something? Why was she acting so strange?

"Are you sure?" The corners of Jersey's mouth twitched, as if she was trying to hold back a smile. "It's refreshing."

Has she put something in the water? Samantha wondered. *Is she trying to poison me?*

She watched in confusion as Jersey unscrewed the cap before offering the bottle again. "Have some," she urged.

"No." Samantha's voice was firmer that time. "Just leave me alone."

She began to shut the door, but Jersey quickly made a jolting movement and tossed the contents of the water bottle at the side of Samantha's face that was still visible through the door frame.

There was a slowed down second where both girls stared at each other; one in bewilderment, and one with self-satisfaction.

And then Samantha's skin started to burn.

Chapter Fourty Nine

She'd never felt pain like it before and she quickly dropped to her knees, screaming in agony whilst Jersey watched her with a sly expression.

It felt like her skin was *melting* and Samantha wanted to claw at her cheek in order to try and get whatever poison it was off of her and stop it from burrowing through her flesh.

Through the haze of pain, her brain whirred with questions about what Jersey could have done to her before she finally remembered all of the news stories she'd read in recent years about acid attacks.

Surely it wasn't that, was it?

As she continued to shout out and roll around the floor in pain, she was vaguely aware of her neighbours coming out of their flats to see what was going on. They watched with horrified looks as she pleaded with them to help her.

"Please. It's burning me. Someone do something."

An older woman stepped a bit closer. "Don't worry, love. Just try and calm down. We've called an ambulance."

Samantha continued to scream. She just wanted someone to distinguish the fire that was consuming her face and neck.

"We've called the police as well," the woman told her. "Given them a description of that girl who ran away so they can catch her."

Her words surprised Samantha.

Jersey had run away? She hadn't even noticed. But then again, she kept on slipping in and out of consciousness so wasn't aware of half of the stuff that was going on.

Each time she opened her eyes it seemed the crowd outside her door had multiplied, and she had no idea how long she had been waiting for help to arrive. It felt like the ambulance was taking hours to arrive, but really it could have only been a few minutes.

When she finally heard the sound of paramedics telling the crowd to disperse so they could get through, she groaned out in relief, thankful that someone was finally going to do something before the rest of her skin had a chance to burn off.

Samantha flinched as she was suddenly doused with a couple of buckets of water before she then felt people cutting her clothes off of her body.

"It's okay. It's okay. You're going to be fine," one of the male paramedics told her as he started to pour smaller amounts of water directly onto her cheek. He turned to his colleagues. "Let's get her to the ambulance."

Samantha moaned as they moved her onto a stretcher and started to roll her out of her flat whilst her nosy neighbours watched with wide eyes.

At some point before they reached the front doors of her building, the pain and fear finally got too much for her and she allowed herself to black out as a way to escape the suffering.

It was a scarily familiar experience when Samantha next opened her eyes and found herself in a stark white hospital room surrounded by beeping machines.

The only difference in her surroundings compared to last time was her mum and dad huddled together at the end of her bed having some kind of tense, whispered conversation.

"Hey," Samantha said to them in a croaky voice. Her mouth felt strange and her words sounded slurred but she assumed it was because of whatever pain relief she'd been given.

As one, her parents turned to look at her with both relief and worry in their eyes.

"You're awake!" her mum exclaimed, rushing to the head of the bed and tentatively picking up Samantha's left hand. "How do you feel?"

"Numb," she mumbled. She oddly didn't feel much of anything, but she was grateful for that because it was better than the alternative of being in as much pain as she'd been in earlier. "How long have I been asleep?"

"Only a couple of hours. The doctors and nurses cleaned your burns and bandaged you up." Elizabeth looked towards her husband. "You should probably go and tell them she's awake." They watched her dad leave the room and then her mum turned back to her. "The doctors will probably want to check your wounds because they're worried about infection. And you'll probably need some more pain relief soon."

"Mum." Samantha interrupted. "How bad is it?"

Her mum gave her a forced smile. "It's bad now, but it will get better. They said they'll give you a skin graft, and you were lucky in a way because your glasses protected your eyes so you don't have to worry about your eyesight or anything."

Samantha felt the urge to cry but the muscles in her face didn't seem to be working so no tears came. "It was acid, wasn't it?" she asked, wanting to confirm what she already knew.

Her mum nodded sadly before perking up again. "But you'll be fine. The doctors are going to look after you, and we're here. You'll get through this."

"Yeah." Samantha was lost in her own thoughts for a moment but then she suddenly remembered something. "What about Jersey? Did the police find her?"

Her mum's expression darkened at just the mention of the girl who had done this to her daughter. "Yeah, they got her. She's been arrested and they said they're going to make sure she goes away for a very long time."

That was a small relief, at least.

"What about Wardell? Does he know?"

"No, sorry. He's called your phone a couple of times but we didn't answer. We thought we'd let you tell him."

Samantha nodded, already starting to worry about having to break the news to her kind of boyfriend, but then a doctor and nurse came into her room and she was soon distracted by their fussing around her and replacing her bandages with fresh ones.

"Can I have a mirror or something?" Samantha asked the doctor. "So I can see my face?"

He exchanged an awkward look with her parents. "It's probably best if we leave that for a day or so. The wounds are still fresh so they look worse than they really are."

"Oh. Okay," she said in a small voice.

The doctor gave her another smile and then left the room, leaving Samantha wondering, *What the hell has Jersey done to me?*

Chapter Fifty

"Do you have my phone?" Samantha asked her mum a short while later. "I'm going to call Wardell."

Her parents left the room, saying they'd give her some space whilst she explained everything to him, and then Samantha took a deep breath and pressed the green button next to his name in her contacts.

She automatically put the mobile up against her right ear as it started to ring, but soon winced when she remembered that was where her injuries were.

"Ah shit," she muttered at the exact same time as she heard Wardell's voice come over the line.

"Hello? Samantha? I can't believe you actually called."

"Err, yeah." She put the phone carefully against the left side of her face. "Sorry. Hi."

"Are you okay? Are you at home? Can I come round?"

"No," she said bluntly, not meaning for it to sound so rude. "Err, I'm not at home. And I'm not even really alright."

"What do you mean?" The concern in his voice made her want to cry before she'd even told him about her attack.

"I'm in the hospital."

"What? Why?" She heard the sound of him grabbing his keys and then a car door slamming a moment later. "Which hospital? What's happened? Did you do something?"

She vaguely wondered if there would ever be a time in her life where she went to hospital and people didn't automatically assume it was because she'd tried to kill herself again.

"No, I didn't do anything," she told him. "Jersey did."

"Jersey?" He sounded panicked. "What did she do?"

"She, erm." She broke off mid sentence, not knowing the proper wording to use. "She...threw acid on me."

There was a deadly silence and then, "Which hospital?"

Samantha told him the name and then he hung up without another word.

She heard a commotion outside her room about fifteen minutes later, and the sound of Wardell and her parents arguing filtered through her door.

"Is she in there?" Wardell asked, panting as if he had run all the way from his car. "Can you please move? I want to see her?"

"I'm not sure that she'll want to see you." her dad said. "It's a bit of a bad time."

"She's my *girlfriend*," Wardell said angrily. "She called me. I assume that means she wants to see me."

"We're not trying to be cruel by stopping you," her mum said. "It's just, it will be a bit of a shock for you to see her. You might want to wait until tomorrow."

"No! I don't care what she looks like. I need to see her!"

He barged his way into the room and then froze as he met Samantha's eyes. "Oh my god."

"Does it look that bad?" she asked timidly. "No one will give me a mirror so I've not seen myself yet."

He schooled his features into a more neutral expression and then approached her bed with a small smile. "No, you look fine. You still look beautiful."

Samantha highly doubted that but she appreciated the lie. "Thanks."

"I can't believe Jersey did this to you. What the fuck happened?"

"We'd like to know that as well," her dad's voice suddenly said. They turned to see both of her parents in the doorway. "I thought the girl who attacked you was just some random nut job who knocked on your door. That's what your neighbours thought. Who was she really?"

Samantha and Wardell exchanged a look, and then she started to tell them all the full story.

"Jersey is another patient of Wardell's. She's a bit obsessed with him, and she didn't like it when she found out we were together so she's been bothering him a lot. But, today, for whatever reason, she decided to come to my flat. Apparently she followed me there one time so knew where I lived. When I answered the door she was acting really weird and calling me ugly and saying she didn't understand why Wardell likes me, but that she was going to make sure he doesn't like me for long. She offered me a drink from what I thought was a bottle of water, and then she threw it on me and...I found out it wasn't really water."

Samantha looked around at the three of them and saw a mixture of rage, horror and disbelief on their faces.

"So this is your fault?" her dad asked, directing the question at Wardell. "That crazy girl attacked my daughter because of *you*?"

Samantha had purposely not told her parents about Wardell's real history with Jersey, but she should have known they would blame him anyway.

"I'm sorry," Wardell said, sounding as though he was barely keeping himself together. "I told Jersey to leave us alone. I thought I'd got rid of her. I had no idea she'd do something like this."

"Well she did!" Her dad suddenly exploded and walked around the bed to square up to Wardell. "That woman has disfigured my daughter. She'll always have the scars from this. She'll never fully recover from what happened. And it's because of *you*. You should have seen this coming. That woman is your patient. You should have known what she was capable of and had her sectioned before she could ever do this. It's all your fault."

"Joe, calm down," her mum said, coming to rest a hand on her husband's shoulder. "There's no point getting angry at anyone except the girl who actually did the attack."

"But I am fucking angry. I wish we'd never met you." He jabbed his finger into Wardell's chest. "I wish we'd never accepted your help. You've just caused one problem after another."

"I know. I'm sorry." Wardell had tears in his eyes. "I was trying to *help* Jersey. I thought I could…" He trailed off.

Thankfully, her dad seemed to have worn himself out and so didn't continue with the argument.

"Why don't we give these two some privacy?" her mum suggested. "They probably need to talk."

He reluctantly agreed and let his wife guide him out of the room, leaving Samantha and Wardell alone.

Chapter Fifty One

"How do you feel?" Wardell asked, breaking the silence.

Samantha shrugged. "I don't really know. I'm not in pain at the moment, but I'm just kind of struggling to process that this has actually happened."

"I'm so sorry Samantha. Your dad's right. This is all my fault. You must hate me even more than you already did." He sank down into the chair beside her bed and put his head in his hands.

"I don't hate you," she told him quietly, tentatively reaching a hand out to rest on his shoulder. He looked up at her. "I'm still upset about what you did, but I don't blame you for this. Jersey chose to attack me because she's mentally unstable. It's no one's fault but hers."

He gave her a grateful smile. "I love you Samantha."

She didn't answer.

"I'm sorry." He sighed. "I'm just trying to let you know that...I'm not going anywhere. I want to help you through this. I want to be there for every stage of your recovery, and I want to keep reminding you that this doesn't change anything. You're still the most beautiful girl I've ever laid eyes on, and burns aren't going to make me feel differently towards you. Okay?"

Samantha nodded after a moment's hesitation. "Okay."

He leaned over and placed his hand over hers, giving it a comforting squeeze. "So, will you stop pushing me away? Will you let me be there for you? Please."

Again, she nodded. "I'm still not sure if I want to be in a relationship with you again though," she told him quietly, not wanting there to be any confusion between them. "And I think, with everything that's happened, I just need to focus on myself and not worry about things like that for a while. I've got too much other stuff going on now, so can we just be friends? At least for the time being? I'll figure everything else out later."

Wardell looked hurt but he gave her a tight smile.

"Yeah, of course. That's fine. We'll be friends."

Chapter Fifty Two

Wardell stayed by her side almost 24/7 after that.

He was there to rearrange her pillows, or to pour her a glass of water, or to do any other thing that she might have needed.

Her parents were being civil with him, and Samantha thought their opinion might have improved slightly, but she knew that they were secretly still annoyed and thought he was interfering.

She wondered if they'd ever fully like him again, but didn't let it bother her too much because all she cared about was that she herself was pleased that he was with her.

The only time he'd left her side was when he quickly went home to get a shower and a change of clothes, and for the hour when the police came to see her to take her statement about what had happened when Jersey came to her flat.

She was grateful he was so keen to help and to show her that he still cared about her. He held her hand whilst the nurses changed her bandages and cleaned her wounds, he slept next to her on that uncomfortable chair and was there when she woke up during the night after a bad dream, and he was there to stop her feeling so alone whilst she tried to deal with the life changing injuries she'd received.

Once she'd been in hospital for almost a week, the doctor finally let her have a mirror so that she could see the full extent of the damage to her face, neck and shoulder. It was the day before she was due to have a skin graft to cover some of the most severely affected flesh, so he thought it would be a good idea for her to see the 'before' so that she could fully appreciate the 'after' the next day.

Wardell, as usual, was beside her holding her hand when the doctor came in with the mirror. Her parents stood on the other side of her, giving her reassuring smiles and telling her to not panic too much because she would look better after the skin graft anyway.

"Are you ready?" the doctor asked in a scarily serious tone once he'd removed her bandage.

Samantha took one last moment to prepare herself and then nodded. "Show me."

He handed her the mirror and she slowly turned it around, feeling Wardell's hand tighten around hers when she let out a gasp at the sight of her reflection.

She couldn't decide if it was better or worse than she had imagined.

The whole right side of her face was red and uneven, making her look like some kind of villain from a sci-fi movie. It was scary to see how close the acid had gotten to her eye, and she was grateful for her glasses which had prevented her from losing her vision.

The skin around her mouth was puckered, causing her lips to tilt down at a strange angle which she hoped wouldn't be permanent. She didn't want to look like she was constantly scowling.

The damage continued down her neck, making her flesh look like raw meat, and Samantha carefully pulled back the neck of her hospital gown to see that her shoulder and the top of her arm also had patches of burned skin.

"Wow," she said quietly, unable to think of another appropriate word at that moment.

"That's probably enough now," Wardell murmured, taking the mirror out of her limp hand and giving it back to the doctor.

Samantha stared blankly ahead, unable to meet anyone's eyes because she didn't want to see the pity that she knew would be there.

It was somehow even worse than when she'd tried to kill herself because the acid attack had been done to her *involuntarily*, whereas she'd chosen to walk in front of Wardell's car of her own free will.

After her suicide attempt, she'd only really had to deal with psychological scars which no one else could see, but the acid burns would remain part of her flesh for the rest of her life; a permanent physical reminder of what had happened, and a reason for any new person she met to start asking questions or to stare at her as if she was some kind of freak.

Just the thought of it was terrifying.

"Can you all leave me alone please?" she asked in an emotionless voice that she didn't think she'd ever used before.

"Oh. Yeah. Okay love." Her mum patted her uninjured shoulder. "We'll come back later."

Her parents and the doctor shuffled out of the room, but Wardell lingered by her bed, trying his best to catch her eye.

"Do you want me to stay?" he asked, probably hoping her request didn't apply to him because she usually always wanted him there.

Samantha shook her head.

"No. I need some time by myself. Please leave."

Chapter Fifty Three

Samantha asked a nurse to make sure that Wardell and her parents weren't allowed into her room for the next three days. She knew they wouldn't be happy about it, and even thought she heard their raised voices outside in the corridor a couple of times, but she felt like she needed some space from them all so that she could wrap her head around the new sort of life that had suddenly been forced on her.

The life of a victim.

Her skin graft operation had gone well apparently, but she hadn't been shown the 'after' reflection yet because the doctors wanted to give it a couple of days to heal and so had put another bandage over her cheek to reduce the chance of it getting infected in the meantime.

"Good news. I think you should be able to go home tomorrow," the doctor told her when he came on one of his regular rounds.

"Really?"

"Yep. We'll give you everything you need to be able to clean and redress your wounds, and I'll sign you off work for a couple more weeks, but other than that I think you should be fine."

"Oh. Cool."

Although Samantha hated being in hospital and had thought of nothing else but wanting to go home for over a week, she suddenly felt terrified at the idea of finally getting to do so.

Once the doctor had left her room, she immediately turned on her mobile and called Wardell.

He answered after only one ring. "Samantha, hey. Are you okay?"

"Err, yeah. Are you busy?"

"No, I'm just at home. I've tried to come and visit you for the past three days, but the nurses always said you didn't want company."

"Yeah, sorry. I told them not to let you in." She could feel his disappointment through the phone, but he didn't say anything more about it.

"Is something wrong?" he asked instead. "Do you need me to come now?"

"Um, do you mind?" She felt awful about the mixed signals she was probably giving him, and she didn't want to come across as if she was using him whenever it suited her, but she was desperate to not be alone right then.

"Of course not." She heard his keys jangling on his end and then the sound of his front door closing. "I'll be there soon."

Whilst she waited for him to arrive, she called her mum, wanting to apologise for seeming rude for the past three days.

"It's fine honey," her mum reassured her. "I know you're going through a lot. How did the skin graft go?"

"It was good, apparently. I've not seen the results yet but the doctors said they're happy."

"Oh good. Maybe it won't look too bad in the end." There was an awkward pause in the conversation. "Anyway, have they mentioned anything about you being able to go home?"

"Err, yeah actually. They said I can get discharged tomorrow."

"That's great!" her mum said cheerfully.

"Yeah."

"Aren't you pleased?"

"Yeah, I am. It will just be weird to go back to my flat after what happened." Samantha didn't admit that her lack of enthusiasm was due to more than just her worries about it being weird. She was actually *scared* to go back there, to the scene of the crime.

"Well, you can always move in with us for a while, if you want," her mum offered. "We'd love to have you back here."

Samantha pulled a face, thankful her mum couldn't see. "Erm, I'll think about it."

Although she had a good relationship with her parents, she didn't particularly like the idea of moving back into her childhood home. She had too many bad memories about living there because it had been where all of her mental health problems had started, and so she worried that if she had to stay there again all her old problems would come back.

She promised her mum she'd call her later that night and then hung up the phone, just as the door to her room opened and a nurse popped her head in.

"Your boyfriend's out here. He said you apparently asked him to come?"

"Oh, yeah." Samantha sat up in her bed. "You can let him in."

Wardell appeared a moment later and smiled widely when he saw her, as if it had been weeks since they'd last set eyes on each other instead of only a few days. "Hey, how've you been?"

She shrugged. "Okay, I suppose. They're giving me less pain relief now though so my face stings a bit."

He winced. "What does it feel like?"

"Like when you've already got sunburn and then you burn yourself again. My skin just feels...odd. I can't really describe it."

He came to sit on the edge of her bed. "What about the skin graft? Was that okay? What does it look like?"

"I don't know yet. They want me to keep the bandage on until at least tomorrow so that it doesn't get infected."

"Do you want me to be here with you when they take it off? Or would you prefer to be alone?"

Samantha placed a hand over his and gave him an appreciative smile. "I'd like it if you were here."

"Good. Then I will be."

"Thanks." She twisted the bedsheets between her hands nervously. "Actually, I'm being discharged tomorrow."

His eyebrows raised and his eyes lit up. "Awesome. Are you excited to go home?"

"Not really."

His face fell and he eyed her with concern. "Why?"

"I'm just kind of....scared."

"Of Jersey? You don't need to be. She's locked up until her trial, and even after that she won't be free for a long time."

"I know." She closed her eyes briefly, embarrassed about having to admit the things that were going on in her mind. "I'm just worried that being back in my flat might give me flashbacks or something. I mean, I don't know that I'll ever feel safe there again, and I hate the idea of being alone. Is that stupid?"

Wardell shook his head. "No, that's not stupid. It's understandable."

She couldn't figure out if they were talking as friends or as patient and therapist, but either way he was making her feel better just with his presence and calm voice.

"I don't suppose, erm." She struggled to get the words out. "Can I, um, stay with you?"

From the shocked expression on his face, she knew it had been the last question he'd expected to hear, but he grinned widely.

"Of course you can. You can stay as long as you want. Forever, if you like."

The smile he gave her was teasing, but the intense look in his eyes told her that his offer was entirely serious.

"We'll see," Samantha said softly.

Chapter Fifty Four

Samantha's mum and dad came to the hospital early the next morning to bring her a bag of some of her clothes and other random things that they'd collected from her flat so that she wouldn't have to go there herself.

"This should last you until the end of the week," her mum told her. "If you want more bringing after that, just let me know."

"Thanks mum."

Samantha changed into a pair of comfortable trousers and one of her favourite t-shirts, sagging in relief once she was free of the hospital gown, and then they sat and waited for the nurse to arrive to remove her bandages and sort out her discharge papers.

"Are you sure you don't want to come and stay with us?" her dad asked whilst they waited. "I mean, you've not really known Wardell that long. Are you sure you'll be comfortable there?"

She rolled her eyes, half expecting him to go on another rant about how what had happened was Wardell's fault. "Yeah, I'll be fine."

Regardless of the unresolved issues that were still lingering between them, Samantha knew that Wardell still loved her and that he would take care of her and keep her safe whilst she was under his roof.

That was all she cared about in her current situation. Everything else faded into insignificance.

As if their conversation had conjured him, Wardell strolled into the room a minute later, twirling his car keys between his fingers. "Morning." He smiled awkwardly at her mum and dad, and then gave Samantha the wide, familiar grin she was used to. "Has the nurse not been yet?"

She shook her head. "No, the doctor told us she'll be here soon though."

'Soon' turned out to be another half an hour which the four of them passed in an uncomfortable silence with only the odd word spoken between them quietly, like patients in a dentist's waiting room scared to talk above a certain level.

"Okay, I'm here," the nurse announced as she entered the room looking flustered. "Let's get that bandage off, shall we? Then I'll give you one last clean and you can get out of here."

She moved Wardell out of the way so that she could stand directly in front of Samantha and show her the items in her hands. "These are for you to take home. Make sure you clean the wounds twice a day, and apply the cream at night. If you think they're getting infected at any point, come back to the hospital and we'll take a look, okay?"

Samantha nodded, taking the different bottles and wipes from her and placing them on top of her bag of clothes.

"Now, let's do this." The overly cheerful nurse looked around the room at her parents and Wardell who had all crowded closer to the bed. "Eager to see the big unveiling, are you?" she joked, immediately making them take an embarrassed step back.

Samantha wanted to tell them to stand behind her so that they wouldn't see her face before she got to, but she refrained herself. She almost wished she could keep the bandage on forever because she hated the thought of everyone examining her in the future as if she was some kind of exhibit showing the effects of acid on human skin.

"Ready?" The nurse asked as her fingers found the edge of the bandage and carefully peeled the corner back. Samantha nodded, signalling for her to continue. "I'll be as gentle as I can." Once the bandage was fully off, the nurse applied the usual creams and liquids and patted the wound dry with a clean cloth. "Do you want to see?"

"Yeah."

The same mirror as last time was lifted in front of her face and Samantha had to blink a few times before she finally accepted that what she saw was the correct reflection.

She was disappointed to realise that she didn't look that much different.

Most of the redness and the damaged tissue was still there for all to see and there were just two small patches of smoother skin at the top of her cheek which still somehow looked out of place.

"Oh," was all she could say as she continued to stare at herself. She hadn't been expecting miracles, but she'd been hoping that they'd have been able to cover more of the scarred flesh than that.

"It looks good, doesn't it?" the nurse said encouragingly.

"Yeah." Samantha forced a smile, noticing how her mouth still seemed to be a strange shape. "It looks good."

Chapter Fifty Five

She was discharged shortly afterwards and then she said a quick goodbye to her parents whilst still in the hospital room before quickly rushing to Wardell's car with her eyes fixed on the floor so that she wouldn't have to see people giving her funny looks.

"Are you okay?" Wardell asked as he climbed in beside her. "I've never seen you move so fast."

She laughed. "Yeah, sorry. I was just eager to get out of there."

They were both quiet on the drive back to his house, and once they arrived Samantha waited for Wardell to get out and unlock his front door before she was willing to leave the safety of the car herself.

"Err, do you want to come and put your stuff away?" Wardell asked her, looking awkward, as he moved towards the staircase.

"Yeah. Sure."

It was only then that she suddenly considered sleeping arrangements for the first time.

Would he think she was sleeping in his bedroom with him?

Did she *want* to do that?

Wardell came to a stop outside one of his two spare rooms. "Which one do you want?"

She knew he was really asking which of the *three* rooms she wanted to stay in, and she looked between them all, pondering what to do and what the repercussions would be of either choice.

Finally, she decided.

"Can I stay with you?" she asked shyly. "I don't really want to sleep alone."

He tried to hide just how pleased he was by her question, but failed miserably. "Yeah, I'd like that." He opened the door to his bedroom and started to clear some space for her in the wardrobe. "You can hang your stuff here, and the bottom two drawers are empty so you can have them."

"Thanks."

Unfortunately, there was a mirror right beside his wardrobe, and she couldn't help but stop and stare at her reflection as she passed it.

"I'll take that down," Wardell offered, reaching for the mirror.

She stopped him. "No, it's fine. Don't worry about it." She turned away and concentrated on unpacking.

"You know you have nothing to be ashamed of, don't you?" Wardell said quietly from behind her. "I've told you, you're still beautiful. A few scars don't change that."

Her chest warmed at his words, and her skin tingled where she could feel him watching her. It was nice to know that, no matter what anybody else thought, Wardell was still there to try and make her feel good about herself.

She stepped towards him and stared deeply into his eyes, seeing the pure sincerity there as he gazed at her in exactly the same way that he had always done in the past.

Nothing had changed for him.

"Make love to me, Wardell," she said softly. "I want you to show me how beautiful you think I am."

His throat moved as he swallowed, and she thought for a second that he might refuse and say that she wasn't in the right headspace for doing something like that. She thought he might tell her to wait until her scars had healed properly.

But he did neither.

Instead, his eyes shone with understanding as he searched her features before settling on her mouth. "Is that what you need?"

Samantha smiled at the huskiness of his voice and nodded slowly. "Yes. I need you Wardell."

His hand came up and carefully cradled the back of her head whilst she parted her lips and sighed as he began to gently kiss her.

Chapter Fifty Six

"Does that hurt?" he asked, pulling away slightly.

She wrapped her arms around his neck to stop him from going any further. "A bit. But it's fine. I just can't move my mouth as much as I used to."

"It's okay," he said with a smile. "It still feels nice."

He put his lips back on hers and started to turn them towards his bed, guiding her to lie down across the mattress as he positioned himself next to her on her uninjured side.

"I want to do something for you first," he murmured. "Okay?"

Samantha nodded, and then held her breath in anticipation as she felt his hand slide down her stomach and push under the waistband of her trousers.

"Ah," she moaned breathily as his finger found the sensitive flesh between her legs and began to rub her.

"Is that good?"

"Yeah. So good."

She could feel his hot breath on her cheek as he started to place soft kisses there. "You're so wet. I love touching you like this."

She parted her legs slightly to give him more room and opened her eyes to see him gazing down at her with a mixture of determination and what she could only describe as devotion.

"I love you Samantha," he told her. "Nothing could ever change the way I feel about you."

She wanted to say the words back to him, but something held her back, telling her to wait a bit longer. "Kiss me again," she told him instead.

He did as she asked and she panted against his mouth as his stroking gradually sped up until she was quivering through an orgasm.

Wardell eagerly undressed them both whilst she tried to control her breathing, and then he sucked one of her nipples into his mouth and swirled his tongue around it as his hips jolted forward and he thrust inside of her body.

"Fuck," he groaned, moving to her other breast whilst his hand came up and kneaded the first. "Are you okay baby? Am I hurting you?"

"No." Samantha pulled him harder against her, somehow enjoying the pain that it caused. "Don't stop."

He made love to her slowly and passionately, taking his time to kiss every inch of her skin that he could reach whilst his hands caressed her. She had never felt so cherished or loved before, and when she finally came in his arms she wasn't surprised to feel a tear rolling down her face.

"That was incredible." Wardell rolled onto his back and ran a hand through his sweaty hair. "Are you alright?"

She smiled at his concern. "Yeah, you don't need to ask me that every five minutes."

"Sorry." He turned onto his side and draped an arm across her stomach. "Samantha, just so you know, if you ever need me to do that for you again, I'm more than happy to. Any place and any time."

She giggled. "I'll hold you to that."

Chapter Fifty Seven

Samantha lost track of how many times they had sex over the next few weeks. It was always at least twice a day, but sometimes could be up to five depending on if she was in a particularly sad or horny mood.

As time went on, her burns started to hurt less and less until eventually they could fuck each other in all sorts of positions without having to worry about it causing her pain.

Wardell got a call from his boss a couple of days after she was discharged from hospital, and was told that his suspension was over and that he could come back to work which he did the following Monday.

He and Samantha started their sessions together again twice a week, but they tended to focus on her attack and how she felt about it instead of her depression and anxiety in general.

Wardell had admitted that he was worried she might try to hurt herself again because of what had happened, so she found that he didn't leave her alone much when he wasn't at work, and was always watching her with concern in his eyes,

She didn't mind though. She liked him being there for her.

When it came time for Samantha to go back to work at the office, she began to have small panic attacks at the idea of having to face everyone there and so Wardell suggested that she quit her job and find one where she could constantly work from home.

"But I don't have any savings," she told him. "I wouldn't have any money."

He shrugged as if that wasn't an issue. "I'll pay for us both."

"You can't do that."

"I don't mind."

She couldn't help but be tempted. "What about my flat, though?"

"What about it? You don't want to live there anymore, do you?"

"Well, no. But I feel like a hindrance being here. It's not fair on you."

Wardell wrapped his arms around her waist and smiled down at her. "I like you being here. I *want* you here. With me."

"Really?"

He laughed. "How can you even doubt that? I tell you I love you about ten times a day."

That was true.

Samantha still hadn't built the courage to say it back to him yet, but thankfully he didn't seem hurt by that.

"So will you stay?" he asked, seeming both hopeful and excited.

She nodded. "I'll stay."

She was only unemployed for a week before she managed to get another role as a remote typist, and she fell in love with the job as soon as she started.

It was nice to not have people watching over her whilst she worked, and to be left to her own devices.

Her employers seemed nice and emailed her regularly to check that she was settling in okay, but other than that they didn't really bother her.

The interview with them had been awkward because she'd had to go on a video call to do it, and she saw the startled looks in their eyes when her disfigured face first popped up on screen, but they hadn't asked her any questions about what had happened and she appreciated that.

Other than that one occasion and the couple of hospital appointments she'd had to go to, Samantha hadn't left Wardell's house or come into contact with other people in almost two months.

She was too scared to do so; not just because she didn't want people to stare at her, but because she had an irrational fear of someone trying to attack her again.

Wardell had offered to take her out a few times but she'd always refused, and when he'd tried to broach the subject during their sessions she'd told him she didn't want to discuss it and he hadn't pushed her.

Still, she could tell that he was worried, and she was starting to get bored of always being inside so in the end *she* was the one to suggest they go somewhere.

"Do you want to go for a walk?" she asked him one Saturday morning as they were lazing in bed.

He turned to smile at her. "Really? Yeah, if you want to."

"Not somewhere too public though," she told him. "Just somewhere with only a few people."

"No problem. I know the perfect place."

He surprised her by putting together a picnic to take with them, and then they set off in his car and drove for about twenty minutes until they finally parked up by a lake she'd never been to before.

"Is this okay?" he asked as they climbed out of the car.

She smiled at the view, and the fact that she could only see two couples nearby who were too distracted by the dogs they were walking. "It's great."

Wardell took hold of her hand and led her through the long grass, over to the section of the lake where all the ducks seemed to be congregated.

"Here you go," he pulled a loaf of bread out of his backpack and they broke it into chunks and threw it into the water, laughing at how the ducks fought each other to be the first to reach a piece.

When one of the dog walking couples passed them, Samantha's natural reaction was to tilt her head down so that they wouldn't see her damaged face, but she quickly admonished herself and forced her head back up, not wanting to be ashamed or embarrassed anymore.

Over the last couple of months her scars had started to heal quite nicely and had just turned to a pinkish colour instead of the shocking red they'd been at first.

Wardell had done his best to help with her self-esteem and, although she still hated what had happened and didn't want people looking at her, she was starting to get to a point where she was able to tell herself not to care.

She would never be able to stop people from judging her or looking at her as if she was some kind of scary monster, but she could make it clear to them that their intrigue didn't bother her.

"Good morning," Wardell said politely as the couple walked by. They returned the greeting and smiled at Samantha, surprisingly not even giving her a second glance.

Wardell winked at her once they'd disappeared and nudged her shoulder teasingly. "Told you you've got nothing to worry about."

She smiled and then continued to watch her boyfriend as he turned back to the lake and threw more bits of bread to the ducks.

They'd been through a lot together in quite a short time, but she was grateful to have him in her life and couldn't imagine being without him.

He was everything to her.

After a few more minutes of her staring, he finally caught her look and raised his eyebrows questioningly. "Are you okay? Do you want me to take you home?"

"No." She shook her head as she felt her love for him expand in her chest. "I want you to marry me."

Epilogue

Four Months Later

Dear Wardell,

I decided to send you this letter because I want to apologise for everything that happened between us.

I've realised now that we were never really soulmates. I was just telling myself that because I wanted to believe it, but I was wrong. I know that now because I've met my REAL soulmate. He's one of the guards here and we're already deeply in love. He's not admitted how he feels yet but I can tell he's just holding himself back because he doesn't want to get in trouble with his bosses. I'm not going to let him deny our destiny forever though (you know how persistent I can be!) and eventually we will be together, whether he likes it or not.

Some parts of being here aren't nice. The food is shit and the other inmates are scary, but he makes everything worth it. He's the love of my life and I'm so glad I did what I did to your girlfriend because otherwise I never would have met him. In a way, she brought us together so thank her for me, okay? I hope she's not holding any grudges towards me because I'm not holding any towards her. We should just be adults and move on from this and be pleased that we've met our one true loves. Right?

I hope you forgive me too Wardell, and that there's no hard feelings between us. I'll always cherish what we shared together and miss talking to you, but I think it's best if we don't keep in contact because I don't want to make my new guy jealous!

Hope you understand that.

Have a nice life!

Jersey
xxxx

Printed in Great Britain
by Amazon